# BLOWN BY THE SAME WIND

Books by John Straley

# BLOWN BY THE SAME WIND

## JOHN STRALEY

SOHO
CRIME

Published by Soho Press
Soho Press, Inc.
227 W 17th Street
New York, NY 10011

Library of Congress Cataloging-in-Publication Data

Names: Straley, John, 1953- author.
Title: Blown by the same wind / John Straley.
Description: New York, NY: Soho Crime, [2022]
Series: The Cecil Younger investigations ; book 4
Identifiers: LCCN 2022022949

ISBN 978-1-64129-527-7
eISBN 978-1-64129-382-2

Subjects: LCGFT: Novels.
Classification: LCC PS3569.T687 B58 2022
DDC 813/.54--dc23/eng/20220516
LC record available at https://lccn.loc.gov/2022022949

Printed in the United States

10 9 8 7 6 5 4 3 2 1

*For my friend Yi-Fu Twan*

*I am carried away by the*
*same wind*
*that blows all these people*
*down the street,*
*like pieces of paper*
*and*

                                  *dead leaves,*

*in all*

             *directions.*

Thomas Merton, *My Argument with the Gestapo*

# 1

## HOW TO DO GOOD IN THE WORLD

It was late spring of 1968 and the abbot of Gethsemane was shaken to the core of his faith. The visit from the FBI agent had given him the final shove he needed to make the dreaded decision, and with that in mind, he sent for the monk to be brought in.

The strong man, the now-famous writer, came in wearing his work clothes, and for all the world he looked like a sun-burned laborer from the fields. The abbot bade him to sit, and then he explained that he very much approved of the brother's travel plans to Alaska, California, and the Orient. He told the brother about the visit from the FBI agent with the unusual name, though he didn't mention Boston Corbett's name, nor the subject of their discussion. It weighed heavy on the abbot's heart that one of his own flock was being investigated as a "radical anti-American subversive." Still, he didn't break the FBI agent's confidence.

The abbot told the tired man, who had just come in from the fields, that even though his writing had brought a great deal of attention to the abbey, this kind of attention from law enforcement was troublesome, and even though he had all faith that the brother was being guided by compassion and the love of God, the abbot wanted the brother to consider a longer absence from the abbey, that perhaps with time and prayer in the wilderness he could come back to the Broth-erhood of the Cistercians. He would always be a brother of the order, but he should consider moving to the new state of Alaska until his heart was settled.

The brother kept his head bowed as he listened. He and the abbot were no strangers to argument. The abbot did not often understand the brother's need to expose so many of his worldly opinions in his writing. But the brother was strong and clearly very experienced. Having come to Christ late in life and grown up with an artistic father in France and England, the brother had a more sensualist worldview than most who were called to the order. If anything, he understood issues of man and culture better than most. His pride was what worried the abbot. There was something in the abbot's tone that made it clear that the brother was receiving a well-considered recommendation and this was not an invitation to argue.

"Some time alone. Perhaps in this place you've been talking about, Cold Storage, Alaska, would be best," the abbot said. "A place where your fame . . . and political opinions have not quite . . . blossomed." He paused and stared at the monk now in a way that left volumes unsaid, but was perfectly understood. The brother patted his dirty hands on the knees of his jeans, then got up slowly with a grimace of pain and left.

THE BROTHER WENT from there and drove the old station wagon several hours through the night to Bowling Green where the young nurse whom he had come to love was waiting for him. M, as he'd refer to her, had cared for him after his back surgery and was staying in a downtown hotel. She was smart and sensitive, and she loved him without restraint. As was pre-arranged, they met alone in his psychiatrist's office. When he told her he was leaving Kentucky, possibly forever, there were tears and passionate kisses that thrilled him and filled him with guilt. Then he said goodbye. Forever.

He drove back to the abbey in the dark, taking a back road

so he could be alone with his thoughts. The headlights of the heavy station wagon tunneled through the darkness. As he reached one of the last crossroads before coming to the unlighted lane leading to the abbey, he saw a barn burning on the hillside. The structure seemed to be rising into the sky on wings, flames flapping up and out between the boards. The smoke resembled a cumulous cloud with a belly that glowed like a shark's.

He stopped and got out, wondering for a moment if there was something he could do, but in his heart he knew there wasn't. He saw the tiny figures of people running in front of the light; soon there would be fire trucks and volunteers from all over the region. Soon there would be relief and eventually a barn raising. But he would be in Alaska by that time.

He was on the side of the road as a dozen cars sped past him turning toward the fire, the brigade of friends and volunteers rushing toward the danger, all for the sake of a neighbor. He stood at the hinges of his car door watching the inexplicable flames and the response of others. His lips moved in silent prayer asking God to have mercy on his sinner's soul.

Brother Louis was in his early fifties. Looking back on this moment from the future, you might be tempted to think that the brother had been aware of his circumstances, fully aware he was just beginning the last eight months of his life, that he would be found dead on a distant floor before Christmas, but there was still so much more for him to do, and God had not given Brother Louis that specific gift of foresight.

Also unknown to either the abbot or Brother Louis, there was revolution in the air even in Cold Storage, Alaska, although the revolution itself still lay in the distant horizon. The little fishing town had a few television sets, but there was no broadcast or cable television, so it was hard to see it coming. But marijuana, long hair on young men, and strange clothes had started to appear with the crews of some fishing boats.

In 1967, *LIFE* magazine had done a story about life in Cold Storage, and people were now coming to visit. Ellie Hobbes and Slippery Wilson had moved up from their original cabin down the inlet and had relocated seven old cannery cabins to the hill behind Ellie's Bar, which they were renting out to tourists. Slippery was taking some of the tourists out on fishing trips and Ellie's niece, Annabelle, would fly them up to lakes in the mountains around the area in one of her two floatplanes. The town itself had one restaurant, and Ellie's would feed breakfast to guests and a few sandwiches at the bar or send some out in the fishing boat. For special high-paying guests, Ellie provided dinner. At night her guests would eat either at the restaurant down the boardwalk or in Ellie's establishment for an additional charge. That first year of '68, the cabins were about a quarter full, and that was fine with everybody involved.

Annabelle had a three-year-old boy named Clive and she sometimes hired girls from up and down the raised plank walkway to watch him because she was scared to death that the little boy would tumble off the plank street and crack his head open on the rocks below. He always had on his old orange life jacket, which was as bulky as a parachute on him, and Slippery suggested Clive wear his old infantryman's helmet, but the child would not countenance it.

The town itself was busy in the summer. The cannery was up and running and boats were lined up at the dock many days to unload fish to be cleaned, canned, and shipped out. The trade of flying out fresh frozen fish or fresh iced-down fish to restaurants was an experiment that was just being considered in places with more boats and better plane ser-vice, but the fishermen knew the day would come when prices climbed and people got the taste for fresh salmon and halibut.

College kids from the Lower 48 still worked cutting fish, and they played the new music in their rooms at night. Some were smoking pot in the woods, and this had some of the old people upset. The boys grew their hair longer than most people were used to, and they had to use hairnets at the cannery. They wore mostly blue work shirts, blue jeans, and flannel jackets. The girls wore all sorts of colorful clothes both at work and off: Mexican blouses and tie-dye skirts. *Sgt. Pepper's Lonely Hearts Club Band* and *Surrealistic Pillow* records came in on floatplanes, and the music washed over the air, along with patchouli oil and marijuana on summer Sundays. Boys who dressed in green army jackets and wore ponytails hanging down their backs walked down the boardwalk with their arms around girls wearing capes, halter tops, and bell-bottoms, turning the heads of the World War II vets, who ran wooden schooners and had heard the stories of free love and endless drugs coming from Southeast Asia.

There had been four instances that summer when someone had broken into a building and stolen a small amount of money and a few items of sentimental value to the owners. Burglary was unknown in town before that summer of 1968, and most of the old people figured it had been brought to town by the new workers at the cannery. There were not just boys with long hair and girls who didn't wear brassieres, but two African American men working at the cannery who immediately jumped to the top of the suspect list.

There was still no road into or out of Cold Storage, but, somehow, in 1968, the world had arrived. In March, Lyndon Johnson announced that he had decided not to run for president. Some said it was because of the Tet Offensive in the first part of the year. Boys from Cold Storage had gone to the war and three of them had died: two Native boys, Charlie Pete and Alex Todd, had been shot on the same afternoon, trying to secure a landing area after being dumped on the ground by a helicopter, and a white boy named Wilson Whitman died when his jet went down, though his parents waited for years to learn if he had been captured. The bodies of Privates Pete and Todd were brought back home on a military barge from Juneau. Captain Whitman's body was never

found. All of the boys had fished with their families and were
memorialized on a hill off the road to the dump.

Glen Andre came back in early spring. He had gone
into the army to learn how to repair radios and somehow
ended up being a door gunner on a helicopter. He had
been a funny kid you could always count on for a joke
or a favor when you needed it. Slippery Wilson would
always call him if he needed a strong back for the day,
and he would show up with a smile and an extra sandwich to share. If someone was sick, Glen would ask after
them, even as a teenager. He would bring over some of his
mom's cookies or some hot soup. He wasn't a showoff—he
just seemed kind like that.

Things changed when he got back in the middle of May
of 1968; he was different. His hair was long and he didn't
speak much. He wore his army jacket with a bronze star
pinned on the front and he slouched at the bar by himself.
He didn't have a steady job but did odd jobs for Slippery.
Some in town suspected he was committing the burglaries
simply because he always had money for a drink. Ellie spoke
to him throughout the day and if some of the old-timers
tried to tease him about his hair or his drinking, she would
wave them off, saying Glen needed his space. Slippery himself had been to war and had run into deep water on Omaha
Beach on D-Day, where he almost drowned with his gear on,
then dragged the body of a kid he had played cards with
that morning as bullets whizzed past them into the wet sand.
Others who had never seen battle said some hard things
about Glen and how he had changed. They said he had
become a hippie and a coward. But Slippery would have
none of that within his hearing, or around his boat or crew.
As far as Slip was concerned, Glen Andre was welcome anywhere in town, no matter what length his hair was.

On April 4, somebody killed Martin Luther King Jr. It
seemed like it must have been a white Southerner who shot
him up on that motel balcony, but it took them a long time

to catch him. There were so few Black residents in Cold Storage, exactly none in the wintertime, and only a few when the cannery was working in the summer. Some called Alaska "the most northern Southern state," and many fishermen were casually racist in their thinking. One old-time fish worker relocated to Petersburg but then moved back quickly, saying, "Hate that town, not a white man to be found; it's almost all Norwegians and Indians." So there was mostly wide-eyed surprise at the reaction to Dr. King's murder. Ellie closed the bar and flew up to a remote lake to be away from the worst of the idle chatter after it happened.

Some Arab kid killed Bobby Kennedy that June, and no one in Cold Storage was exactly sure why. Someone said it was because of something Kennedy said about Israel. That kid didn't make it far at all. Rosey Grier tackled him right there in the kitchen of the fancy hotel in California. This came closer to home for most of the people along the board-walk. When Arabs start killing white men, even if they were Catholics, this was something to pay attention to.

In August the Democratic convention in Chicago turned into a violent television show everyone watched. That's when everyone's self-righteousness started overflowing into the streets and the hippies started calling policemen "pigs." Even people in Bush, Alaska, started getting pissed off about people with long hair again.

Now, all these things had an effect on village life, but none as much as the deaths of the boys in the war. Or the drowning that happened in the spring when Kyle Burton's long-liner went down. The weather was bad, but back then the short openings were scheduled a long time in advance, and when the allocated fish were caught, the season ended, so people rarely stayed in on account of the weather. If you didn't go out, you were not going to make any money. Kyle went out in his old boat, and when he turned to come home, the seas broke on the stern, and the boards around his rudder opened up, sending green water to flood his engine room. His crewman got into his survival suit, but Kyle's tore open and he died of hypothermia before help arrived.

In a fishing village, this news is more real than the Chicago Seven, or Sirhan Sirhan's motive for murdering a man running for president. Everyone in town could imagine the sound of the engine sputtering out. Everyone knew the smell of diesel fuel in seawater and the cracking of planking as an old boat twists into the seas. The sea insinuates itself into your dreams and into your waking.

In 1968, Ellie had hosted her share of funeral receptions at her bar. She often kept the leftover flowers around for the pleasant smell. Most people brought wildflowers or simple flowers that grew easily in their gardens next to the mountainside: rhododendrons, fuchsia, bachelor's buttons, or irises. Children sometimes would bring armloads of pussy willows if a death occurred in spring. Ellie's Bar had a fine old rosewood bar and a few round tables, but there was also a twenty-foot-long yellow cedar table that Slippery had made for buffets that he kept along the rear wall where people often sat to watch the pool games near the back door.

Ellie was sixty-one years old in '68, and she was still as strong as she had been the day in the '30s when she and her niece rowed up the Inside Passage with Slippery Wilson and landed in Juneau during the mine strike. From there they rowed to the outer coast where the old-timers were just building a town near a hot spring. George Hanson, the Seattle cop who had been following them up the coast, had ended up staying in Cold Storage as well. George had pretty much given up police work, but he served as a deputy for the federal marshals when anything had been needed in territorial days. In statehood, he still had a good relationship with the troopers, and they would let him make citizen's arrests out in the villages if anything got too frisky and if he didn't take credit for anything important, which was fine with George. George had asked around town about the burglaries, and he, too, suspected a couple of the cannery workers, but he had no proof and none was likely to come in the form of physical evidence, because there was no way to dust for fingerprints or get footprint impressions. The troopers did not like to waste time traveling out to the little villages to take prints from a scene that would be trampled through by almost everybody in town before the weather let them fly into the area. George just recommended that people lock their doors if they were really worried about it. But no matter how much people fretted about hippies and "coloreds" creeping through their houses, most people didn't bother locking up. They just kept their rifles by their beds with one in the chamber and the safety off.

Summer meant time out on the water, and George would take the burglaries seriously in the fall when the cannery workers had left town. If things went missing after that, it meant one of the locals was involved. It would be easy enough to find them when they got to drinking hard and one of their buddies snitched them off. He would then get them to return the little trinkets and pay the money back.

George, however, was beginning to feel old and tired of wrestling people around, so he wasn't very hungry to make arrests or get the court system involved. He didn't want to be a cop anymore. George much preferred running his con-verted schooner, hauling goods up and down the coast to the little villages, bringing hay and grain to the few farmers who kept cows, and groceries to the fox farms on the islands. He had a good solid hold in his boat and a stout launch to run goods ashore when needed. Mostly, George just liked puttering up and down the coast exploring the anchorages, dropping in a line to catch halibut, and shooting a deer from the deck when one presented itself on a near shore. He traveled with a mongrel hound dog named Dot who slept in the wheelhouse with him and would wake him anytime she heard the anchor chain dragging. Dot weighed in at around a hundred pounds, which was about twice too big for a boat dog, but she was attentive and had learned to poop over the back deck and pee into the scuppers, so she was considered a good sea dog by most everyone in the fleet. She also seemed to enjoy surviving on sour milk and halibut, of which George seemed to have an endless supply.

It was almost the last day of August when Annabelle walked from her small office at the harbor ramp down to Ellie's Bar. She had one flight that afternoon and wanted to check with Ellie to make sure that her passenger had a room for the night. Annabelle had been the little girl with the yellow bird when they rowed up the Inside Passage in 1935, and they had lost the bird somewhere just north of an old cannery in British Columbia. Annabelle still missed that damn bird. It was Ellie who had been crazy about flying an airplane, and in fact Ellie had bought the first plane, the de Havilland Beaver, and had taught the girl to fly. But it was Annabelle who started Buddy's Flying Service back in 1958, when she was thirty-one. Annabelle was forty-one now and the business was doing fine. Ellie flew for her sometimes, and she hired a couple of kids as ramp rats to carry gear and shipping supplies up and down from the dock. She also hired a full-time mechanic, who lived part-time in Juneau and part-time in Cold Storage. Annabelle was very finicky about the planes and their upkeep. She would not let a second tick past their mandated inspection time, and she liked to keep them looking and sounding good because she knew greasy old planes scared people more than dumb-looking pilots.

It was about ten in the morning and the bar smelled of the big pot of fresh-brewed coffee. It was the second pot, for Slippery had made the first one for his new group of fishermen, who had come in from Alabama just the day before. Glen was sitting down at the end of the bar, his dark hair hanging down over his eyes. Ellie was playing James Taylor on the record player.

"Hey, girl," Annabelle said to her aunt. She laid her ball cap on the bar, and her braids tumbled onto her shoulders. "How's business?"

Ellie looked all around the bar and then back to Glen, who was the only customer. "We are having a special today for veterans of foreign wars: free coffee!"

Glen looked up and smiled at Annabelle, then pushed his coffee cup forward for Ellie to top it.

"Hey, Glen," Annabelle said, "you want to come down to my office later and take a look at my single sideband radio?"

"What's wrong with it?" he said without much enthusiasm.

"I'm not really sure. I know they sound screwy normally, but it seems to be cutting in and out, and you know there are a lot of logging camps starting up and a bunch of them need flights. I could get some money out of them while they are here. I thought I should have a good coms link with them and none have called me yet."

"You want me to look?" he said in a flat voice, as if he were just waking up.

"Yeah, you know, with all your government experience."

"With all my government experience I could go down to your office and shoot the radios with a fifty-caliber machine gun." He took a sip of the coffee. "Come on, Ellie, can't I have some brandy in this?"

"Not until noon, sweetie." Ellie smiled at him.

"I know you know about radios, you lunkhead." Annabelle squeezed his broad forearm.

"Okay . . ." he said.

"Listen, El . . . I have one man flying in from Juneau this afternoon. He just gave his name as Louis. Says he is staying with you. Do you have him down?"

Ellie Hobbes scanned the few names written on her new-looking register. "Yep, that's what I have. He wrote to me from a place in Kentucky . . . Gethsemane, Kentucky. He's some kind of religious person. He gave his name as Brother Louis."

"Huh? A priest?" Annabelle said.

"Naw," Glen said, "a monk, I betcha."

"I'm not sure I ever met a monk," Ellie said. "He wrote

me a letter and said that he is looking for an isolated place to stay for a while where he can write and read and be away from the rest of the world. I told him about our old cabin site."

"You think he's a fugitive?" Annabelle asked her aunt.

"No more than we are, darlin'," Ellie said.

"I thought you didn't care much for holy rollers," commented Annabelle, who knew almost too much about her aunt's old political views.

"Aw . . ." the old radical organizer said, "I got no problem with this new breed of 'em if they keep their noses out of my business and aren't a bunch of temperance biddies."

"Well, I just hope to Christ he has a cask of brandy with him," Glen said.

"There ya go, boy," Ellie said, and she poured a shot of brandy into Glen's coffee.

"Hey, thanks, El."

"Heck . . . it's noon somewhere."

The women laughed. Annabelle picked up her hat, tucked in her braids, waved, and headed out the door into the sunny morning.

# 2
## BROTHER LOUIS

Although that August of 1968 had been relatively dry, in the beginning of the third week a slight low-pressure system moved in from the southwest with fifteen-mile-an-hour winds, causing moderate turbulence from sea level to fifteen hundred feet. But because of the clouds, the ceiling came down to seven hundred feet.

Brother Louis was anxious about flying. He had very little experience in small airplanes, let alone planes that took off and landed on the water. He had been disoriented ever since he left Kentucky. He had been planning this trip for two years, and at first he assumed it was going to be an out-and-back adventure, an opportunity to be in a remote location where he would be left alone to meditate and write. Someplace where his readers could not just drop in on him. But now he was not sure what he wanted. After his last talk with the abbot, he was feeling more like he had been exiled. He had traveled to Anchorage and around Juneau. He had met the nuns of the Catholic Church who spent their new lives teaching Native children, yet Alaska felt forbidding. Mountains rose straight up from the sea, with their rock walls and summer snowfields. The landscape was largely vertical, hard and cold. He became more and more aware that he was a heartbroken old man, soft and warm-blooded in a world of hard surfaces. God seemed to have His hands out like a traffic cop commanding pilgrims to stop and reconsider their path. He had imagined this as a trip to find other like-minded pilgrims, but the more he saw of the country the more he felt like a refugee.

Then there was his problem with the FBI. They had certainly frightened his abbot, but Brother Louis doubted the country's top law enforcement agency would follow him to Alaska. He was not a criminal. He was a writer.

Annabelle walked from behind the wooden desk she shared with other pilots in the Juneau airfield. She had some papers in her hand, and her braids still poked through her ball cap.

"Louis?" She stood over him.

"Ah . . . yes," he said as if waking from a troubled sleep.

"Good. You want to go to Cold Storage? This way." She pointed to a door to the airfield. She didn't wait for his answer. He simply walked behind her as if he had no choice in the matter.

The flight from Juneau was not particularly rough, but it took a bit longer because Annabelle had to stay out of the inland passages as she followed the coast down. There were just a few bumps. She looked over at the brother once she had cleared the floatplane pond, then rose up above the islands to the west. She had just the one passenger: a surprisingly handsome man with short hair who appeared to be very fit and in his early fifties. When he looked at the map, he put on his horn-rimmed reading glasses. He was wearing a plaid shirt and blue jeans under a dark navy coat. She had half been expecting a fat man in a long robe eating a big loaf of bread and chugging a jug of wine, but instead this man looked like Ken Kesey when he smiled: big shoulders and strong arms. He had only one bag and a briefcase, which he carried, and a nice-looking camera, which he used quite often during the flight. He had many questions about the islands—who lived on them and how people survived. Annabelle did her best to answer his questions, but the engine noise made it difficult. They stopped to deliver mail in

Pelican and the brother wanted to run around the town for a bit, but she asked him to stay close because they were not going to be there long. Brother Louis snapped a few photographs and asked her how she came into the country. When she told the story of her aunt and the Industrial Workers of the World, about the police chasing them and the policeman staying to live alongside them in the little roadless fishing town, Brother Louis was fascinated and could hardly contain himself from asking even more questions. Questions that Annabelle cut off by grabbing Pelican's small pouch of outgoing mail to Cold Storage and starting the engine.

It was just a twenty-minute flight down the coast to get to Cold Storage. Annabelle circled over the town and buzzed the boardwalk. Then she flew a bit south and circled the little harbor with the grass flats up next to the steep mountain where Slippery and Ellie's old cabin sat. This time of year there was a small coho salmon run, and two brown bears were fishing in the stream that ran near the cabin. Rain was falling now, and as the de Havilland Beaver banked hard to turn back toward town, Annabelle pointed down and yelled over the engine noise, "That's the cabin I grew up in. That's Ellie's old place she told you about." Brother Louis took another photo and then looked up with a broad smile.

"The bears . . . are they always there?" he yelled as she pulled back on the power and leveled out, pumping the flaps.

"Naw," she said, "mostly just when the fish are around. They won't bother you when they are eating fish. You got a gun?"

He shook his head as if it were something he had never considered.

"We'll take care of ya." Annabelle smiled, powered down even more, and began to put the floats on the water near the harbor.

ELLIE'S BAR HAD a small outdoor counter built under the eaves of the roof, and the bartender could serve five customers seated outside while they tended the bar inside. A sliding window kept things dry when the weather blew in hard. It wasn't quite legal because the outside bar was reserved mostly for kids, who were not allowed into bars anytime alcohol was being served. But Ellie was sick of answering phone calls from kids asking permission for all kinds of ridiculous nonsense from their drunken parents, and refused to take responsibility for passing on instructions—or worse, lying—to children about their parents' wishes. So it was well known that if a child came to Ellie's any time of the day or night they could sit outside, rap on the window, and Ellie would give them a glass of soda, and they could talk to whomever they wanted. Sometimes Ellie had cookies for which she might charge a dime, but real store-bought candy bars went for full price. Ellie was stingy about those because she was worried about most of the kids' teeth. She cut them off after two sodas, then served them ice water and sweet cherries after that.

The day Brother Louis walked into Ellie's and set down his bag, Glen was sitting drinking his usual coffee and brandy, wearing his army jacket, and Ellie was letting him play her newest Lovin' Spoonful album. Glen was nodding along with "Summer in the City." Sitting on a high stool at the outside bar was a sixteen-year-old girl who was about to turn seventeen. She was blond and wore a short neon red-and-green tie-dyed dress with a thick rope of cheap wooden beads around her neck. Her hair seemed the color of spun gold and hung down her back uncombed but looked to be freshly washed. A person would be forgiven for being confused about how old she was because the girl herself seemed to be confused about her age. It seemed she had grown to maturity in just a matter of weeks. Yet most of her gestures and expressions were still childish.

Slippery and George, who was Ellie's oldest and best friend, had recently commented on Venus's development, telling Ellie she needed to keep an eye on her before a rascal high school boy married her. Ellie had ignored them, but deep down inside she knew there was some truth to their words.

"BROTHER LOUIS, I'M Ellie Hobbes. I run the place, the bar and the cabins. My man Slippery runs the boat. I'm sure you'll be seeing him around. Good to meet you." She put her hand out and he shook it. The brother looked down and noticed her left hand. She was missing two fingers completely and half of her middle finger. He couldn't help wincing, though the stumps seemed to be healthy and well healed.

*He has kind eyes,* Ellie thought, but the type of tightness around them suggested he was feeling some pain.

"It's very good to meet you," he said in a resonant voice.

Did he have an accent of some kind? Ellie couldn't be sure. Maybe eastern? Maybe Southern? Maybe he was just one of those intelligent fellas.

"Are you the kind of brother who can stand a drink before dinner?" she asked, and here Glen looked up at him.

"What are others having?" He looked around.

"I'm drinking brandy," Glen said.

"I've got 7UP," the young woman from outside said.

Brother Louis scratched his chin and looked around. "Well, after that flight over the mountains, I'm awful tempted to have a brandy with you, friend, but I think I will have what the lady is having. But could I buy a round for everyone?"

They all smiled as Brother Louis walked over to the end of the bar, where he was close to the open window and could get a good look at Glen.

The girl had her back to the rain just as the sun broke through the clouds. A rainbow showed over her head and the sun glowed behind her face. It was hard not to be stunned by her looks. She had both the angelic beauty of a Renaissance painting and the earthly sensuality of a much more worldly woman, but folded in on top of all that, she had the goofy body language of a child as she spun around on the barstool kicking her dirty bare feet and staring at the stranger in town.

"My name is Louis," he said, holding out his hand first to the girl and then to Glen.

"My name is Venus!" the girl shouted, twisting her hair. "That's my real name too. Some people think I made it up, but I didn't. Venus. Venus Myrtle." And she stopped her spinning to stare at him, so he could tell that her eyes were a bluish green.

"I'm Glen Andre," Glen said. Then he paused, looked up, and asked, "So are you a Franciscan?"

The brother smiled and said, "No, I'm a Trappist brother, a Cistercian actually. A brother of the Abbey of Gethsemane in Kentucky."

"What's a brother do?" Venus called out, while Ellie put another soda in front of her. The girl was clearly excited to have an exotic visitor in town. "Is it a job? Like a priest?" she almost yelled.

"Wait a minute, baby. Remember, you can use your inside voice sitting here. He's just right close, okay?" Ellie said.

Venus shrugged, blushing. "Sorry . . ." she said, and she was.

"That's all right. Yes, being a Trappist is a job. It's really one of the greatest jobs anyone can have."

"Whattaya DO?" Again, she almost yelled, and again she was embarrassed. "What do you do?" she repeated in a small voice.

"We live together, and we do our best to love God, but more than that we do our best to be happy while doing it."

"Why?" Venus asked softly this time.

"Because we hope if we do it successfully, if we can sustain ourselves loving God, if God sustains us and other people see how happy we are, then we hope that inspires others to love God as well."

"That is SO COOL!" Here Venus couldn't contain herself.

"Oh, yeah, just groovy," Glen said, picking up his brandy glass, downing it in one gulp, and putting it softly down. "It's nice work if you can get it, I suppose. I got to be going, folks. Thanks for the drink, Brother."

Then he was gone.

The remaining three were silent for a moment.

"He's troubled . . ." Ellie began to explain.

"No, that's okay. I do put people off sometimes. I wasn't going to introduce myself by the name I use in the abbey. Like I say, it puts people off, but I'm afraid I was a little charmed by your enthusiasm, Venus . . . Which is a perfect name for you, by the way."

"Thank you. Do you have another name?" she asked.

"I do . . . but I will only tell you about it later when I'm getting ready to leave. Okay?" He smiled at her and held his finger to his mouth as if he were telling her to hush, then he turned to Ellie. "Perhaps you could show me the cabin and I could take a look around before dinner?"

Thinking he would want quiet, Ellie took him to the cabin farthest from the bar, down the boardwalk, up some stairs, and down a narrow trail. At the cabin site there was a covered porch that overlooked the inlet down toward the south, where their old cabin property was. The newer cabin Brother Louis was to stay in was made of plywood, but it was sturdy. The trees around it were ancient and there was hardly any undergrowth. The small building itself still sat on the original heavy log skids, but large spruce stumps had been added to level it off. The decking had been built over berry bushes, and there were ripe berries for the picking within easy reach. An old Adirondack chair sat next to a small table, both positioned to afford a view down the inlet.

"This is perfect," he said, "thank you," and he opened the door where the double bed, woodstove, sink, and closet sat waiting. He looked at the gas cookstove and told her that he had plenty of experience with them before she even asked.

Ellie explained that the water from the sink was rainwater

from a catchment system built on a platform up the hill, and the outhouse was just ten yards past the cabin on the trail. She asked him to please not put any garbage down the hole but to bring it down to the bar, and she would take care of it.

Brother Louis bowed to her and said, "Of course. This is lovely . . . really."

"Here is your key," Ellie said, placing it on the small table. "It works on both the front and back door." The key was attached to a red-and-white fishing bobber to keep it afloat in case someone dropped it off the boardwalk at high tide. "We had some kids sneaking around and getting into some of the businesses. They don't take much, but if you have anything valuable, I'd lock it up. They haven't broken into any windows or doors yet, so I don't think we are dealing with any criminal masterminds. I just wanted you to know."

"Thank you. I don't imagine there is much crime around town, is there?" The brother sat on the edge of the bed.

"Not the kind of crime anyone wants to talk about. Just the things that men do to their own family members. I suppose you have that in the South, don't you, Brother? Babies being left alone when parents are on a bender. Women walking around town with black eyes no one wants to ask them about."

"Yes, I know what you mean, Mrs. Hobbes."

"I love this town, Brother, but if you are really thinking of spending time here, I wouldn't want you to come with an idealized impression of tranquility."

"No, ma'am," the brother said.

"Tomorrow, if you want, we can go out to the old cabin site to see if you might like to stay longer."

"Yes." He leaned back on the bed and motioned for Ellie to sit in the chair by the inside table, one of the three straight-backed chairs available.

"I didn't know how many chairs you would want, Brother," she said. "Mr. Thoreau said that if you had three in a cabin this small you were inviting all of society in."

"I might move one outside, so I can have companions in either place. But I don't have to worry about society."

"My niece wonders if you are a fugitive," Ellie said with a straight face.

"Really?"

"I'm not sure if she is really worried." Now Ellie smiled— just a little. "But we are sometimes suspicious up here. Single men who want to be all alone are not all that common. Single men that call pretty young girls 'charming,' when they are technically of age but still too young to marry." Ellie took a deep breath. "These men that carry bottles in their bags but won't drink at the bar." Ellie pointed directly at the brother's bag. "Not to put too fine a point on it, Brother, but I've known some men of the cloth I wouldn't trust as far as I could throw them . . . particularly around a bottle of booze, a pretty girl . . . or boy for that matter."

"Your instincts aren't wrong, Mrs. Hobbes." Brother Louis was smiling and looking her straight in the eyes. "You should be protective of that girl. I assure you I will do whatever I can to earn your trust." He leaned over and took his bag off the floor and put it on the bed next to him. Then he unbuckled the straps and unzipped the fat zipper. He pulled out a quart bottle with a homemade label and a brown pharmacist's-style cap. "This is liniment. It's what you heard glugging in my bag. It was made for me by one of the sisters in Anchorage. She is a Yupik woman, and she says it is made from the roots of a plant that grows along the river by her village. I don't doubt that it has some alcohol and DMSO, and even some canning wax in it. I have terrible back pain, you see, and she recommends that I warm some of this up as hot as I can stand, soak a rag with it, and put it on my back at night. I tried it last night in Juneau, and I'm not sure if it went to my nerve pain, or if the smell went straight to my head, but I slept very well."

"Well, good. We will give you some of our own home rem- edies if that doesn't work. And I'm sorry. I'm a bar owner and not one to judge anyone for sin. Particularly you. I don't mean to be unfriendly. I'm just . . . I just look out for Venus. She doesn't know what effect she has on boys yet, and her parents, well, they are okay, but they are 'modern,' you know."

"Yes," Louis said, "and I don't mean to be mysterious with her. You see, I am looking for a place to be alone. I'm serious about the contemplative life. I love my brothers, and I love the practice of prayer and serving God in the way we do, but—"

"You fell off the wagon?" she asked, trying to be sympathetic.

"Not exactly," he said, putting the liniment back in his bag but not zipping it up. "I was a writer before I joined the brothers of the abbey. And you see, we each work to support the community. Your niece told me about you and the Wobblies. 'Each to their ability to give, and each in their need to receive.' That is what I admire about the Marxist philosophy, see? I happen to think that the only place the communal philosophy of Communism really works is in the monastic community, and possibly only there. At least so far as—or because of—love . . . See?" He looked at her again, not wanting to offend. "Well, anyway, my abbot wanted me to write a book about how I came to my faith and came to the abbey, so I did! And it was a hit! Now all the money goes to the abbot."

"So I can see why you left. That's not fair."

"No!" he said, probably more loudly than he intended. "I was fine with where the money went. In fact, it was perfect. But now, see? I was this famous monk and people started writing to me. They wanted to visit me." He slapped his hand on top of his head. "It was a nightmare."

"Being famous? I hate to tell you, but I've never heard of you." Ellie was smiling, beginning to feel sorry again for this poor, crazy man.

"That's because I'm here under my formal name I use at

the abbey. I don't want to have it all start again if I find a new place to write and pray and live a contemplative life."

"Are you a Marxist or one of these radicals? Is that your problem?"

"Not really, but I am deeply opposed to the killing that is going on in this war in Vietnam. I have been in communication with people all around the world, some of them in Asia, about their traditions and their ways of worship, and I'm convinced that we have more in common with them than we think. They want peace. I'm certain that they love creation and their god the way we do, and they are much more successful in inspiring people of their countries to practice this love than we are. Now I talk about all this with writers and thinkers, and it's not that popular. I get harassed by some people, some of the . . . the young people call them *squares*, see? What that means is people who want to force something natural and organic into an artificial or man-made form."

"So you are a hippie?" Ellie slapped him on the knee.

"Sadly without the drugs or free love, Mrs. Hobbes."

"I can't have you walking around calling me Mrs. Hobbes. Please, just call me Ellie, or Comrade Hobbes if you have to give me a title."

"Is Slippery your husband? Not that it is my business."

"We have been together a long time." Ellie smiled and her face lit up in the way someone's does when they have nothing to hide. "Once when Annabelle had to get some student loans for college down at the University of Washington, she absolutely needed some information about her parents. Both of them were long dead. I could get the information about my sister, but the father was long gone and we would have had to go down to Montana and probably hire a detective to dig up the information, so it was easier to just get married in Juneau and hire a lawyer to adopt Annabelle with her full consent. Then we could apply for the loans. I don't wear a wedding ring because"—she lifted up her injured hand—"I got my mitt chewed up in a lathe when I was working in a fish plant in the thirties."

"I noticed. That must have been painful." Brother Louis nodded to her hand and returned her smile, grateful that she was so open.

"Yeah, not too bad, really. I mean, right when it happened." She paused, looking now at her hand. "Later it hurt like a bastard, until I found a doctor in a Ketchikan whorehouse who treated me well. The cannery people couldn't have cared less." They both stood there looking at the hand in silence as if they were expecting it to speak.

Ellie cleared her throat. "So we got married but didn't do any of the name stuff. We stayed at a nice hotel and drank champagne and had sex a lot, so I guess you could say we are hippies too."

"Well, good," Brother Louis said. "Even us sinners can love God and do good for the children. Isn't that right, comrade?"

"And the workers. Speaking of which, I better get back to the bar. Some of my customers may be serving themselves by now. Again, don't make too much of Glen. He just got back from the war, and I think he's hurting pretty bad. I used to be like him. I didn't want to hear anything about God for a good long time."

"And now?" he asked.

"I just judge the people who flop up at my feet. As long as they seem all right and try to be good and fair, then they are all right with me. And so, God is taking care of things just fine." She looked around the cabin slowly, her gaze lingering on his bag resting on the bed. "So, anyway"—she pointed at the key—"we don't usually lock doors around here, except for the recent incidents. Always little things, nothing major."

"Someone must know who it is, and I don't imagine secrets are easy to keep around here. I've lived in villages before, and neighbors, even if they are two miles away, seem to know everything," the brother said while he picked up the room key.

"Yes," she said, "there is a lot of talk. What worries me is how people run their mouths about Glen just because he has changed so much from being in that war."

"How has he changed?" The brother looked at her damaged left hand for some reason.

"He's been deeply hurt. He used to have a sparkle in his eye and enthusiasm for hunting and fishing and, you know, Brother, for life."

"And that seems to be gone?"

"Yes, but that doesn't mean he steals things, does it? Although some people seem to think so."

"Would you mind if I try gently to find out what is hurting the boy so badly?"

"If he doesn't snap your head off. The accusations from folks around town make Glen grumpy."

"Who do you think it is, then?" the brother asked.

"Oh . . . I don't know. Whoever is doing it takes cash. They robbed my bar of some cash, then they went upstairs into our house. They took some cheap jewelry and went through some drawers but didn't trash anything. They took some scarfs and stuff. I can't see a grown man like Glen doing that. The jewelry wasn't worth anything, and besides, there is no place to sell it. They robbed the Cold Storage office of money and some old photos. Glen . . . well, I could see him breaking things up, acting out, but not sneaking around. Like I said, he's grumpy and will snap at people. Not a cat burglar type, I'm thinking. Just don't get into a fight with him. He's got a world of hurt in him, and he's liable to put some hurt on you."

"Oh, I'm not worried. I've been snapped at plenty. It's not all peace and love inside an abbey." Then he took out his liniment and started to unpack.

# 3
## VENUS

Brother Louis opened the door to the cabin and peeked out. The rain was still falling. He put on a waxed canvas jacket and a wool cap and made it back down to the bar before the fishermen returned. Venus was still at her post at the outside bar. He sat down next to her and noticed that she was now wearing jeans and a fisherman's sweater, along with rubber boots and a ball cap.

"I'm gonna eat dinner and then do a short shift at the cannery." She smiled at Louis as she pulled her hair into a ponytail with a colorful elastic. "They make us wear these dumb hats. I think it makes me look like an old lady!" She made a pouting face.

"Probably better than getting hair in one of the cans of fish."

"Yeah . . ." She yawned.

"Are you going to eat here at Ellie's? What about your parents, don't you eat together?"

"Not tonight. My dad is practicing with his band, and Mom is doing transcendental meditation."

"Ah," Louis said, not wanting to interview the child.

"I have my own account at the restaurant, but Ellie lets me eat for free when she has a lot of guests if I help her set the tables and then do dishes after my shift."

"After? How long is your shift?"

She spun around and around on the outside stool using

his stool to kick off from, in a motion that seemed well practiced. "Oh, they're only letting me work two hours tonight. I will just work the lift and help unload two boats. Once I help unload, another guy runs the ice machine, and I might run some errands for the guys on the boat. Go to the store, buy candy, but I can't buy beer or whiskey no matter what. Even if they give me a note. I can buy cigarettes with a note sometimes. But the storekeeper has to know the guy. They say that if they ever see me smoking I will lose my job, but yuck, I don't want to smoke. Who wants to smoke, anyway?"

"That's a good choice. I used to smoke when I was young. I didn't brush my teeth and I drank alcohol as well, and look how many teeth I had taken out." He opened his mouth wide and used his index finger to pull his cheek down to show her.

"Gross!" she squealed.

"Gross, indeed," he said.

"Where did you grow up that you didn't brush your teeth? Didn't your parents make you? Mine do, every night."

"I grew up in lots of places. Mostly England and France. Then America. My parents died when I was pretty young. First my mother and then my father. I lived with my father mostly in France."

"What did he do in France?" She stopped spinning and looked at him intensely, trying to imagine a life as exotic as France.

"My father was a painter," he said.

"Really . . . that's so cool! Wow! A painter in France. Did he paint naked ladies and stuff?"

"Oh yes. Naked ladies, naked men, but mostly landscapes and cities. He loved old buildings, and he loved trying to capture light and color. He was a good painter and had some important shows. But he never became famous, you know, like Van Gogh or Monet."

"Oh . . ." she said.

They both stared out toward the harbor. The rain from the eaves made a Pissarro painting out of their view. They both stayed quiet—Brother Louis not wanting go any further into his father's painting and Venus not wanting to talk about how she didn't know who Van Gogh or Monet were.

"There's Slippery's boat!" she said as she pointed, and he saw a fine forty-foot wooden boat slide on the mirrored water into the harbor. A young man untangled the bowlines and then worked his way down the port side and put down two bumpers to protect the boat while it was tied up at the dock. The blond girl used two fingers in her mouth to blow a loud whistle, then waved her hand high over her head. Slippery Wilson opened the narrow side door next to the helm and returned the girl's wave with one strong arm.

Brother Louis looked at her and tears came briefly to his eyes upon seeing how beautiful and open she was. God must have blessed her to put her here in this lovely place where people obviously looked out for her.

Men tied the boat and the deckhand used a handcart to bring a green cooler full of salmon and halibut up the dock. The two guests carried their fishing rods along with them while they laughed, and one lit two cigars—one for each of them.

At first appearance, both men seemed like happy tourists: one was fat and the other was thin and lanky. The lanky one wore his beard and a distinctly Southern mustache, Van Dyke–style, and the fat one was clean-shaven. They both had deep Southern accents.

"Why, hello, darlin'," the first Southern gentleman said as he walked up to the bar. "You really should have come along. We got into 'em today."

"Good for you," Venus said, her face beaming. "I had to stay home and do chores."

"You're a good girl. I could see that the moment I laid eyes on you," the fat one said, and he gave her a hard side-arm hug. He put his cigar back in his mouth and extended a big hand to Brother Louis. "I'm George Atzerodt," he said. "My friends in Birmingham, Alabama, call me Atz, though."

"Well, good. I'm Brother Louis from Gethsemane, Kentucky."

"You a fisherman, Brother?" Mr. Atzerodt asked.

"I've done a little stream fishing, and I pulled some lobster pots in my time."

"Well, we had a fine time on the ocean today, I tell you. We started turning them loose."

The other man put out his hand. "Ed Spangler. I been up to Gethsemane one time. Bought some bread and a fruitcake for my mama. They put whiskey in it up there. Darn good."

"Yes, sir, it is."

"We didn't miss supper, did we?" the other asked as he hurried past to look in the bar.

"No, sir. I believe Ellie was waiting for some of Mr. Slippery's fish," the brother said, and the gentlemen waved their fishing caps like rodeo cowboys and bounded up the stairs to their cabins with great brio.

"Oh, don't you just love summer?" Venus spun around on her boots this time and gave a little hop. "Company all the time. Interesting company from such interesting places like France and Birmingham, Alabama." She shrugged and stopped to look at the brother's face to make sure that he felt the same sense of wonder.

Ellie stuck her head out of the bar door and said, "Venus, the tables look beautiful. You did a great job setting them. But the Cold Storage called and they need you down there pronto to unload those boats, so you better skittle skattle."

Venus was off running like a young colt before Ellie finished her sentence. The brother watched her disappear around a corner of the boardwalk.

"Brother, would you mind helping Glen pull that cooler of fish up the ramp? It's low tide, and I'm betting it's heavy and the boy might dawdle. I want to get some of that fish cooking."

"Of course." He began walking quickly down the boardwalk toward the harbor.

The little town was made of small wooden houses. Some of the houses on the mountainside had short pilings down to the tide flat and some even had small gardens cut into the slope of the mountain. Fireweed was in bloom then, as were bluebells. Several houses had fuchsia plants hanging by their doors. Next to one, a very large man with a shiny chin and thick glasses sat shucking clams raw, popping one out of three straight into his mouth. Brother Louis listened to the man slurp and grunt the clam down the way he imagined a bear would.

As the brother walked by, the man smiled at him and said, "Hello, sir!" The brother waved and returned the greeting as he noticed the large drift of clamshells that were piled like snow in front of the happy man's little house and continued all the way down to the beach below. Some people had pots out in their yards to gather rainwater, some had little birdbaths with spinning wheels. One had a couple of outboard motors bolted onto boards with their propellers dunked into garbage cans and their engine covers off, and tools scattered on a picnic table. One greenhouse with mildewed paint had a large spruce tree in the back with a mobile made of old rusted chainsaw motors swinging from the limbs.

The houses on the water side seemed in much better condition and had nice boats pulled up underneath and some kind of railroad system to help carry the boats up above the tide. These were small skiffs that ran on outboards. Some of these homes had crab pots stacked on the decks around the house. Some had larger sections of glazed-in windows and big woodpiles under sound shingled roofs, not soggy canvas tarps. Some of the lots even had tent platforms for people who came out for short visits and set up their wall tents, then took hot baths and built fires, played cards and drank with their friends, and ate abalone, crab, salmon, and clams until they had their fill.

The brother made it to the ramp just as Glen was drinking

his second beer while sitting on the cooler at the bottom. He was looking up the ramp, which was indeed steep.

"You want some help with that?" the brother called down.

"The beer? Hell, no!" Glen shouted back. "You could help me think of a way to get this sonofabitch up the hill without breaking my back though."

Louis used his hands on the railing to slide-walk his way down to water level. At a very low tide the boats in the harbor were more than twenty feet lower than they were when it was high tide. There wasn't an extreme tide change now in August, but still, the ramp was steep.

"Shall we pray about it?" Glen asked.

"Unless one of us has a weak heart and might die of a heart attack . . . I don't think it would help." Louis rapped on the old green cooler.

"Or maybe God would bring us a helicopter with a sling," Glen said.

"True," Brother Louis said. "Maybe you should start on that, but I don't want to miss dinner."

They smiled at each other and stood up at the same time. The cooler was tied up with manilla rope rigged around both ends and sides to keep the fish from flopping out. Glen pulled and Brother Louis pushed. Without taking any stops, they got to the top of the ramp with the fish. Once on the level, they each lifted the rigging around the cooler with one hand and easily made it to the bar.

THE GUESTS DRANK as Ellie and Slippery cooked the fish. Slippery came in from cleaning up the kitchen and shook hands with the brother quickly, then brought him some soda water and lime. The two Southern gentlemen had brought some of their own bourbon, offered it around, and sat to drink before dinner. It was just the three of them drinking by the stove, eating smoked salmon and saltines before supper. They went through the pleasantries of travel arrangements and weather. All of them were vague about how long they were staying in Cold Storage, but Brother Louis did mention he had to be in San Francisco in ten days' time.

Atzerodt had a way of lounging in a wooden chair that gave the impression he was the kind of lazy man who enjoyed sprawling out wherever he landed: a country store or a bar room. He had a big head, which made his eyes seem small, but his oddly shaped face, made so by a prominent double chin, was expressive.

"Do you mind if I ask an indelicate question, Brother? I'm just curious about Catholics is all."

Mr. Atzerodt leaned forward while Mr. Spangler put another log into the stove.

"No . . . go ahead."

"Where do Catholics stand on the Negra question?" Here he took a sip from his glass and leaned back, as did Mr. Spangler.

"What question is that?" the brother asked.

"Well, certainly, sir, you acknowledge after what we've seen recently there is a war coming. Where will the Catholics stand?"

"War? You mean the Vietnam War?"

Atzerodt picked up the small splitting axe and cut a bit of kindling from the dry hemlock stick sitting on the stone hearth, more or less simply to add emphasis to his words. He already smelled of whiskey, and just the little effort with the axe made him sweat.

"No, sir!" he said firmly and cracked the stick in two. "The war with the coloreds, the coloreds and the Communists, with their long hair and such. You saw it in Chicago. What will the pope tell you to do? Who will you fight for?"

The brother sat back, a little surprised. "I suppose we would do what our conscience tells us to do and pray as hard as we can, then work for peace."

"Surely, Brother, we are past that. Look at what happened when they killed their supposed leader—the minister. They nearly burned down a dozen cities."

"I prefer to remember how Robert Kennedy kept the peace that night by reading a poem. Reminding the crowd how he had lost a brother to violence, and they listened to him."

"A fellow Communist," Spangler, the thin man, said, "just like his brother, gave up Cuba without a fight," and he brushed the whiskey off his mustache.

"And a Catholic." Atz looked at the brother. No one spoke for several awkward moments.

"But, oh . . . my mother always said to me, 'Edman, never talk politics before dinner, because it will ruin your digestion and the flavor of the food,' and we surely mustn't do that tonight because we have some of the finest fresh salmon and halibut to look forward to eating. I apologize, sir. I certainly meant no offense."

"No . . ." Atz said, staring into the brown murk of his third drink of bourbon. Glen came in from washing up and the two men instantly offered him a big glass of whiskey, which he happily took.

Brother Louis excused himself to go peek in the back kitchen, where he asked if there was anything he could do. Ellie put him to work chopping fresh carrots from a neighbor's garden.

"You talk with the other guests?" Slippery motioned his head to the other room.

"Yes." Louis nodded. "Ah . . . how can I say this charitably?"

"Peckerwoods, I think my father would have called them," Slippery said. "I'm trying my best keeping them quiet around Ellie. I don't want an all-out war at the dinner table."

"Oh . . . I don't think that will happen. I've lived in the South long enough. These types of men like to drink and converse. They don't much mind ruffling some feathers, but usually they want to leave with their charm intact."

"And their views," Ellie grumbled. "Luckily for me, I will be cooking and taking an unreasonable amount of their money as the good capitalist I have become." She looked at the carrots and smiled at the brother, then took the bowl from him. "I have some dressing in the cooler on the porch. It's my own oil and vinegar. Would you grab it for me, Brother?" Which he did.

Outside, the clouds were dark over the water. Brother Louis stopped to look at a large bald eagle sitting on top of a boat's trolling poles and heard the yawping of a blue heron taking off over a sand flat down the inlet. Again he had a moment of wonder at the peacefulness of this tightly packed little town in the wilderness.

Back at the table, the Southerners were asking Glen about his upbringing there in the little town. Glen was doing his best to be outgoing. He talked about the basketball teams and how some years the teachers had to play to make up a full practice squad, or the tallest girls would play opposite the starting team. He talked about his dream to become a radio repair technician and his desire to learn about technology, since it seemed to him that there would be a lot of jobs in the future for people to work on machines.

The Southerners seemed to be of the belief that "working on machines drained a man of independence." They freely expressed their opinions that working on assembly lines, in and around machines, was better left to "the Japs, because they have an aptitude for it and a will to be part of their cultural 'herd,' so to speak."

Glen looked at them as if he had been doused in cold water for a second, then he went on. "Well, I guess I don't know about that, but I know they are going to make a heck of a lot of cars, motorcycles, and electronics in the next few years."

"And let the little gooks have 'em, is what I say." Mr. Spangler toasted Mr. Atzerodt, and just then, as if on cue, Slippery called them to the table.

The fish was steaming on a platter, alongside a big bowl of rice, roasted garden vegetables, and hot biscuits and butter. The Southerners gave out a little whoop and stood behind their chairs.

"Isn't the missus. going to join us?" Mr. Spangler asked Slippery, who was still wearing an apron and looking over the table to make sure everything was out.

"Ah . . . no, she is working on dessert and the coffee. She rarely eats out here. She is always busy."

"Ah . . ." Mr. Atzerodt said as he rubbed his hands together. He had a fat man's hands and slightly effeminate hand gestures. "Well . . . then, Father, ah . . . Brother, sorry, would you like to say the blessing?"

There was an awkward silence and Brother Louis looked at Slippery, who held his hands up to the brother as if to say, "Take it away." Then Brother Louis said a brief prayer asking for gratitude for the food and the labor that went into it, then when he was about to end, he added the final verse of Psalm 19:

"Let the words of my mouth, and the meditation of my heart, be acceptable in thy sight. O Lord, my rock and my redeemer."

The food was so good the conversation quieted down considerably. Slippery brought out a bowl of lemons for those who wanted citrus on their grilled salmon, and a wonderful hot white sauce for the halibut. The Southerners spoke nothing but compliments and only drank cold water during the meal. Glen was the only one to drink a cold beer, but the brother could tell he enjoyed the meal immensely. At one point he saw Glen's eyes sparkle with tears, and as he was sitting close to the young man, he leaned over and whispered, "It's good food, isn't it?"

Glen nodded. "I sure missed it," he said in a broken voice. "There were times I thought I would never get to taste real food again."

"I know exactly what you mean," Brother Louis said, and patted Glen's shoulder. "I'm grateful too to be here with you."

Glen looked puzzled, but he smiled and picked up his beer can and toasted the brother's glass of rainwater.

"Now, not to be accused of beating a dead horse, but, Mr. Wilson, sir, let me ask you, what kind of engine is in that fine boat of yours we fished on today?" Mr. Spangler asked.

"That's a Caterpillar marine diesel," Slippery answered.

"Now, didn't I tell you that was a big old hunk of American iron?" Mr. Spangler turned to his smiling friend. "I knew it first thing when you started it up. That's what I'm talking about, son." He looked at Glen. "Let the gooks have their little bitty cars and their motorcycles. Let them have their electronic crap. Boy, didn't you get a little—and I can say this with no ladies present at the table—but didn't you get a little bit aroused when you heard that big old American engine banging beneath your feet?"

Glen laughed, and even Brother Louis smiled.

"No, I'm serious, son. America makes big iron and plants big crops—corn, wheat, cotton, soybeans. Let the Chinks plant their rice. Let them wade in the water to pound out the little bitty grains to make a meal. Now, please don't get me wrong, this was a wonderful meal, and I love myself some rice as well, but only with good Alaskan fish caught by a white man on his beautiful American boat. Am I right?"

"Well, sir," Glen said.

"SLIP!" Ellie's voice cracked through the door like a thunderbolt. "THERE IS DESSERT OUT HERE."

And sure enough, there was an amazing warm meringue confection with homemade vanilla ice cream baked inside it. Slippery brought it out and laid it in front of Mr. Atzerodt, along with a serving knife. Then suddenly Venus appeared with the plates and set them down beside the serving knife.

She smiled at Atzerodt and said, "I was told to tell you to stop talking and serve the dessert before it melts inside."

Everyone laughed. Then Slippery came out with a tray of after-dinner liqueurs and small brandy glasses, as well as instructions from Ellie to get them talking about anything but culture and politics.

Again, the conversation was circumvented by the food

and drink. Venus ate her dinner back in the kitchen with
Ellie. Ellie did not talk much about her guests, but she let it
be known that she didn't think much of their opinions. Still,
she kept one ear cocked toward the crack in the door so as
not to miss a word they said.

Soon after the dessert was eaten, the Southerners called
Ellie out of the kitchen and began a round of applause for
her cooking. As she came in, all five men stood, making it
a standing ovation. Mr. Spangler stroked his mustache and
toasted Ellie for the fine meal and complimented her for
her hard work and her "diligence in the kitchen." He said
something about how the armies of the world all moved on
love and the promise of a good hearth at home to return to,
and he looked at Glen. Then he pulled up a chair for her and
poured her a glass of huckleberry cordial.

Ellie sat down. She was uneasy, expecting they would once
again start talking some kind of nonsense about race, but
suddenly the conversation turned to an unexpected subject.

"Now, Mrs. Hobbes, my friend and I have been traveling
all through the west. You see, we are on somewhat of a quest."
Mr. Spangler looked down at Mr. Atzerodt, and his friend
nodded to him as if to give him permission to continue.
"You see, it's not completely by chance that we came to your
delightful establishment. We were sent here by providence."

"Really?" Ellie said, and just as she took a sip of the cordial
she had made, Venus came out of the kitchen with young
Clive. They both snuggled in next to Ellie and started eating
from one large serving of Baked Alaska.

"Yes, ma'am. You see, we had an occasion to visit the old
Haywood Saloon down in Aberdeen recently. A place where
I understand you used to work in your youth and that once
belonged to your father."

"You are right, sir, but that was long ago." She looked
around nervously, wondering where this was going. She
stared at the brother, but he shrugged, indicating he had
no idea what the real subject was. So, she continued. "I was a

barmaid in Aberdeen. I was almost as young as Venus, a little older. It was a logger's bar back then, a post office, meeting hall, all-around center for woods workers, back when the trees were falling like stalks of wheat in those woods."

"You would be surprised what it looks like now, Mrs. Hobbes. It's been all tarted up like a dance hall girl. I believe they serve warm ice-cream cones and sell sunscreen over the bar to tourists on their way to the beaches up by the Indian reservations. Not the romantic place that you remember."

"What took you, gentlemen, to Aberdeen?" Brother Louis asked as he watched Venus spooning the sweet cream into the baby's mouth and scooping the runoff up the side of his smile.

"Well, sir, it's kind of an archeological interest of ours. Mrs. Hobbes, do you happen to remember an old, preserved body that used to be on display at the Haywood Saloon back when you worked there?"

"The Old General?" Ellie leaned forward and put her glass down. "My Lord, you men can't be interested in that old thing?"

"Well, yes, ma'am, we are." Both men stared at her without speaking for several long moments. Outside, Annabelle's floatplane could be heard idling down out of the air until its floats splashed into the water. Glen looked at the brother as the pause became awkward.

Venus and Clive had moved on to licking their plate and were paying no attention at all to the adults. Venus picked up a cloth napkin, dunked it in a water glass, and started wiping the boy's face, starting under his nose, which was particularly slippery.

"Well . . ." Mr. Spangler said, "do you know anything about the whereabouts of the Old General?"

Ellie stared at the men as if they both must be crazy. Then she smiled broadly and turned to Venus. "Baby, go get those two kerosene torches and that box of matches out in the pantry and let's go show them the Old General."

# 4
# THE OLD GENERAL

Toward the mountain side of the bar was a concrete tower-like bunker with one set of stairs that led down into an underground area that Ellie and Slip used as a root cellar. Back in 1968, the glaciers churned off enough ice farther out near Bartlett Cove that crabbers would bring Ellie blue chunks of ice along with the occasional delivery of Dungeness crab from the bay. The ice would sometimes last for months, and during the summer, the bar liked to serve beef that they had hung in the cellar. Mostly it all went to either steaks or hamburgers. Potatoes and onions were kept down there also. Ellie and Slip had raised everything out at their original place, but now with them working all the time, it was cheaper to keep one cow a year and feed it, then eat mostly fish and crab and whatever else came in. But often it was a steak or a burger that a fisherman craved after months rolling around in the fish slime.

It had been years ago when the new proprietors of the Haywood Saloon had contacted Ellie about the Old General. It hadn't been unusual back in the day to have morbid curiosities in workingmen's bars. They were the havens of tough and mostly brutal men living brutal lives. Some bars claimed to have the pickled heads of famous Indian fighters, or the preserved testicles of men put to death by the state. There were several bars in the Midwest that claimed to have the penis of the well-endowed Clyde Barrow in a gallon pickle jar. So having a mummy on display didn't shock Ellie's sensibility. It's just that having grown up with it, she didn't really want a fleshy preserved body lying about into her dotage with the people she considered her children and grandchildren around. Her life had changed over the years, and even though she was ambivalent about keeping it around, she didn't want to see the Old General just thrown out with the trash. She was sure there were some fishermen who would buy the old mummy a drink and pose for a picture with a cigarette in its mouth and a drink cupped in its leathery dead hand.

The Old General didn't smell bad. If he smelled like anything at all, it was some kind of old hair tonic. He had been so pickled over the years that God knows what was on him now. He wasn't offensive, even though he was naked. His hands were posed over his shriveled manhood, and his face was not all that sunken and ghostly. If anything, his skin bore the appearance of an expensive and well-oiled leather traveling bag that a salesman might carry.

The owners of the refurbished Haywood had offered to sell the Old General back to Ellie. She had him shipped up on the barge. He was really quite shrunken and weighed next to nothing, so the shipping cost was minimal. She thought there was something appropriate about having the Old General back—it was a tie to her past, when she had last worked across a bar.

There were rumors when she was young that he had been Butch Cassidy, and his body had been smuggled back from Bolivia by a madam in Colorado. There had been other rumors that he was one of General Custer's lieutenants, but the mummy still had his scalp, so the drinkers at the Haywood never took to that story. The story of origin from the man who had traded it to her father for an old sheepherder's wagon was that he had bought it at a railway auction as a piece of unclaimed baggage. Her father called him "Old General" because of his bushy mustache and his serious demeanor.

◎ ◎ ◎

THE GIRL BROUGHT the lanterns. Slippery had meant to wire the root cellar with lights but was suspicious that the lights would keep the heat up in there and spoil the food. The Old General was wrapped in plastic on the top shelf. Holding the first lantern, Ellie led the way followed by the rest of the company, with Slippery coming last with the second lamp. Venus stayed behind with Clive. She had seen the mummy many times. In fact, when she was a child, she and her friends had dared each other various times to sneak down to the cellar and climb up on the shelf and peek into the dead man's eyes. Several times Ellie had brought the Old General out for Halloween and made the children reach over him to get their candy, until some parents objected. Though she mostly found his presence to be macabre, so the Old General only came out once or twice a year.

There were boxes of fish and a side of beef left hanging from a hook in the ten-by-sixteen-foot room. There was a long thick plank table for cutting meat along the wall opposite the shelving. Slippery and Ellie stood on the bottom shelf and grabbed the plastic shroud and hefted the Old General down, then placed it on a clean piece of butcher paper laid out on the table. No one spoke. Atz had brought down a bottle of his own bourbon, and before they removed the plastic, he looked at his partner in the gloom, raised an eyebrow, and took a swig as if for good luck.

They opened it up with no particular flourish, just as if they were unwrapping a cut of meat. But both Southerners let out grunts and looked at each other.

"My goodness," was all Mr. Atzerodt said.

Mr. Spangler took a flashlight from his fisherman's jacket and illuminated the mummy's face. It was a doll's face staring off into the middle distance of nothing, somewhat toward its feet. His mustache was thin, but the hair on his head was evident and brown, perhaps a lighter brown than it had been in life. The flesh on his chest and thighs was shriveled and creased like dried meat, which of course it was. Spangler shone the beam of light down on the legs.

"Look at the markings below the right knee," he said almost breathlessly.

"And look at the left leg. The first report said it was his right leg that was broken, but look at how withered his left leg is. This man clearly suffered a serious injury to it long before he died." Atzerodt took out a small hand loupe to magnify the skin below the right eyebrow. "Hold the light steady, please, sir." He was talking to his friend, who was having a hard time holding the light steady, but his voice was tense and had taken on a strange formality. "Right!" he said. "That is an amazing piece, Mrs. Hobbes. What do you know about it other than all the bar talk that I'm sure you heard over the years?"

"All I know for sure is that my father traded a wagon for the mummy, and my father told me that the man said he got the mummy from a railroad company lost baggage sale around 1920."

Even in the dim light the Southerners' faces seemed to turn pale.

"Holy. Fucking. Christ!" Mr. Spangler said under his breath. Then, quickly, "Excuse my French, Mrs. . . . Brother."

AFTER THEY ALL went upstairs, Venus, Ellie, and Slip did dishes in the kitchen while little Clive sat at a chair at the counter chewing on a piece of bread and drinking from a tall plastic glass of rainwater. The men sat outside under the eaves along the boardwalk. Glen drank from a can of Olympia beer while the Southerners drank champagne as they smoked another cigar. Brother Louis sipped on a cup of hot herbal tea.

"You seemed excited by something looking at the Old General, or am I mistaken?" Brother Louis asked.

"We have been looking a long time, sir, and we will

probably look a long time more before we have our country back," Mr. Spangler said. Spangler's bony face and high cheekbones focused a hard stare down his nose, as if he were aiming a gun at the brother. Then, in a moment, as if remembering his manners, Spangler smiled.

The men smoking the cigars and drinking were clearly happy now, sitting back on the bench. The clouds in the inlet were moving quickly to the south and sunlight was traveling like a train behind them, sparking the water and the tops of the rippled surface with flashes of silver. Glen was drowsy and leaning back with his eyes closed.

"Tell me, please," the brother asked, "what is this country you speak of? What place do Black people, Native people, Mexicans have in your country?"

Both of them chuckled, and Mr. Spangler touched the ash of his cigar to the heel of his boot, causing the burnt column to fall off in a gray chunk.

"Brother, I know you are used to moral superiority, and, honestly, I don't hold it against you. You belong to an ancient institution, which protects you at all costs. It used to protect the white ruling classes of Europe for hundreds of years. It gave it structure during the Dark Ages. The structure of feudalism you love to decry in the old South was originally shaped by your church, until it corrupted itself too much and the Germans had to allow the people back into the equation of the relationship with God."

"Well . . . I think we could argue history there . . ." Brother Louis sipped his tea.

"Of course," Mr. Atzerodt broke in, "but you asked about the country we speak of. It's not so much different from the one you aspire to, Brother. The South wanted peace. It is a fecund and beautiful country. We grew what we needed, and we had a self-sustaining culture and heritage. Say what you will about how the North treated its workers in its sweatshops and factories. Did you read Sinclair Lewis's *The Jungle*? Do you think those workers wanted to live like that in those slums? Do you think the Negras want to live in Harlem in New York City, or in the Fillmore District of San Francisco?"

The brother, who had almost gone to work in a cooperative school for Black children in Harlem before he took his first confession, did not speak.

"Of course not," Spangler said, blowing a big ring of smoke. "Now, it could be said that we should not have brought in a foreign and admittedly such a fragilely inferior race as the Africans. We may have been better off using the Celtic Irish early on, so that slowly we could have assimilated the indentured workforce more seamlessly into our own culture and heritage. Surely we could have handled the labor problems better."

Atz piped up. "We shouldn't have split up families, that was a mistake, and we shouldn't have emasculated the bucks the way we did. Why, it was against our own interests as it turned out. Breaking the will of the menfolk caused a lethargy in the whole herd so to speak. This entire myth of Negra laziness was of our own making, though I hate to say it."

Glen opened his eyes. "I served with a lot of Negroes. One of 'em saved my life in a fight. He was a good man and a good soldier. He got a Silver Star. What you are saying sounds like a lot of shit." Then he closed his eyes again.

"Do not get me wrong, son," Spangler said. "In a way, you are making my point for me. Individually the Black man is hardworking, courageous, loyal, and a boon companion, but I will bet you dollars to doughnuts, boy, that once they got together back at the base or in camp, they were nothing but a bunch of lazy colored boys . . . and that same man who had saved your life wouldn't lift a finger to help you. Am I right?"

Clearly Glen didn't want to participate in an argument along these lines. "Fuck off," was all he said. Then he added, "Excuse my French."

"So let's get back to the country you envision," the brother said.

Raising his glass of champagne, Spangler said, "It will be

a homogenous community as envisioned by the founding fathers. It will be guided by the concepts of the Constitution of the United States. It will be administered by white property owners again, whose first priority will be the stewardship of the land and the Christian values that the founding fathers envisioned. The founding fathers were European white men who read the Holy Scripture, though they did not take their marching orders from the corrupt king in Rome. No offense, Brother."

Louis simply bowed his head, then asked, "But again, gentlemen, what of the others? The non-white landowners—what is to become of them?"

Atzerodt put down his glass, and in the manner of a man who was tired of being polite for far too long, said, "Don't think that we don't notice your tone, Brother. But should I remind you that it wasn't that long ago that your brothers and your church were supportive of a plan in Europe under Mr. Hitler and his National Socialists to be far more brutal to the non-whites and the Jews than anything we have suggested here. So I'd thank you to keep your tone civil, if you please."

"Forgive me, sir, and, no, I'm not unaware of the sins of the Catholic Church. But continue. How do you envision it?"

They both sat back and, by way of accepting his apology, they raised their champagne glasses in a toast to him. Then Atzerodt continued. "Everyone will be welcome to work on the land and to participate in the culture and heritage of the state. The people most suited to making the decisions will make them within the framework of the Constitution."

"And freedom?" Brother Louis asked.

"We have freedom now, and what does it mean? Does it bring peace and happiness, Brother, or does it bring rioting? We don't allow unlimited freedom now, and neither will we allow it in the new state. We will encourage freedom that allows consistency with core beliefs: the protection of private ownership of the land, the protection of racial purity and racial identity, which if you listen to the voices of the people, is what the modern Negra wants as well. We will want community control of its own culture, heritage, and religion. You see, there is nothing scary in any of it. We all want the same thing—good wages, reasonable prices, and happy families."

"To happy families!" Spangler said, and he toasted his friend, and they emptied the last of their glasses.

Then Venus walked out with a tray with mugs of hot coffee. The Southerners grabbed the mugs and quickly poured some bourbon along with a topping of cream.

Atz then scooped Venus up into his arms and kissed her on the cheek as he sat her on his lap. Not that there was much room for her to sit, since most of the space had been taken up by his belly. His arms, however, appeared strong as he squeezed her into his bulk.

"Oh, man, oh, man, I could just eat you up, darlin'."

The girl squealed but did not seem to struggle too much. She settled down into his lap and put her head on the man's shoulder for a moment as if he were going to read her a story. Glen's eyes were open now, and he stared hard at the man.

"Ah . . . Venus, isn't it time for you to get home?" The brother was clearing his throat nervously.

"Nawww, she don't have to get home." Now it was clear to everyone that Mr. Atzerodt was more drunk than he had been letting on. "Naw . . . she is fine right here," and he started kissing her neck.

Venus started to resist, presumably because the man's breath smelled of alcohol and cigars as much as anything. She elbowed him in the chest hard and Atz's little hand grabbed her wrist roughly.

"She doesn't like it," was all the brother heard, and Glen was up, standing over the Southerner slumped down on the bench with the girl.

"Come on now, boy. You keeping her all to yourself here? Is that it? She your reward for making it home in one piece?"

Glen started hitting the man repeatedly with his right

fist. Venus gave a shriek and Brother Louis pulled her from the man's lap and up into his own arms, where Venus was now crying and clinging to his neck. Glen started to employ both hands, beating both sides of Mr. Atzerodt's jaw. Glen's fists slapped hard and Mr. Atzerodt grunted. His champagne flute broke on the decking of the boardwalk. A single bloody tooth fell with the shattered glass.

Then Spangler stood up and held a small .45 Colt derringer to Glen's temple and said in a gentle voice, "That's enough now, son. Atz, here, is sorry for the disrespect he has shown you and this girl. Aren't you, pal."

Atz shook his bloody face up and down in agreement.

"Well, all right. We will say our goodnights then." He uncocked the hammer on the old-fashioned-looking derringer and lowered it to his side. He held on to his friend's arm and helped him up, then backed away, keeping his gun out and ready.

"No hard feelings now. You tell the young lady when she calms down that the whiskey was to blame for his bad manners, and we will make it up to her. All right?"

Glen took a sudden step toward the men, but Brother Louis put his hand on Glen's shoulder and said, "We will pass on your apologies, sir," and with that, the two men walked away.

Venus turned to Glen with tears streaming down her face. "Glennie, are you all right? You gonna get in trouble?" She started blubbering like a baby and fell crying into Glen's arms. Brother Louis watched as Glen started crying in the hard embrace, his bleeding hands gripping Venus's back, his face in the saddle of her shoulder and neck.

Ellie and Slip walked out onto the boardwalk and looked at the scene, but their concerned eyes were drawn up and past the brother.

"Ellie? Venus . . . what the hell is going on here? What are you doing making out at the bar with Glen?"

The brother turned around and saw a man wearing a

patchwork vest and dungarees over red rubber boots. His longish hair poked out from under a dirty fisherman's hat similar to an English driving cap, and he was red-faced with anger or alcohol, perhaps both. "What the hell, Ellie? Has Venus become your bar girl?"

The brother turned around and offered the angry man his hand. "I'm Brother Louis. If you like, I can explain."

"I'm Bobby Myrtle, Venus's father, and I can't wait to hear your story, pal."

# 5
# OUT OF CHAOS

The next morning Annabelle flew the Southerners up to Lake Elfendahl on the west coast of Chichagof Island. Not much was said about the fight the night before. Glen and Brother Louis had made brief apologies to Mr. Myrtle, but Venus's father was not having any of it. He had led his daughter away by the elbow down the boardwalk, and there was no expectation that anyone would be seeing young Venus up at the bar or in Glen's company anytime soon.

At breakfast, Slippery offered to take the brother out to their old property in the skiff and drop him off at their cabin. Glen had offered to bring a large-caliber bear gun in case the brother was anxious about the bears along the stream, which the brother was grateful to Glen for.

Louis had been upset, both by the nature of the Southerners' politics as well as by the whole lurid nature of their examination of the mummy.

"They offered to take the thing off our hands," Slippery said that morning as he was clearing off the table. Slippery was the entire early-morning breakfast crew. He would cook and serve the breakfast, then pile the dirty dishes up to be done later. "There was no big pressure. They just acted like they were kind of apologizing for their behavior. Sort of like they were offering to do us a favor by taking it off our hands, but, still, I could tell they wanted the Old General . . . bad."

"Did they mention a price?" Glen asked as he downed

a third cup of coffee. Ellie had passed down the word that
Glen was cut off from alcohol completely.

"No, they just mentioned we could make a few bucks, and
for us just to think of what we might want . . . It's weird, don't
you think?"

"I have a suspicion about what they are up to," Brother
Louis said softly, "but I don't want to say anything. I might
be wrong. I'd hate to cast aspersions . . . but I might just look
in an encyclopedia if there is one in town."

"Sure, we have a little library down at the school. The
community keeps it running for everyone. I can get it open
for you, maybe after we come back," Slippery said.

After some discussion, they agreed for Glen to take
Brother Louis in his tin skiff to make things easier. Before
they were off, Slippery explained the ins and outs of the
locks and hiding places for keys and special things for Glen
to show the brother.

Glen's tin skiff seemed incredibly light and unstable to
the brother, but fortunately the weather was calm. The little
engine started on the third pull, and once out of the harbor,
its wake was a widening V down the inlet. Gulls rose ahead of
them like collections of dust and several beat their wings just
a few feet above Glen's and Louis's heads as they slid along
the water's surface. Occasionally they passed through a pool
of fragrant warm air that carried the smell of evergreen trees
or damp earth. Once they could smell woodsmoke drifting
across the inlet.

The clouds along the surface of the water were like
shredded cotton, floating above the water and mean-
dering up the sides of the mountains, becoming even more
shredded by the trees. Ducks dove right in front of them
and reappeared in the wash of the little propeller. White
waterfalls splashed down the mountainsides higher than sky-
scrapers. Soon enough a long grassy peninsula jutted out
into the inlet. They went wide to the west to curve around
it, then turned east to head into the crook in the arm, back

under the shadow of the mountain. A smaller fall of a substantial stream could be seen up a narrow valley where seven
Alaskan brown bears were scrambling after coho salmon.

Glen slowed the engine and they drifted against the current. The Alaskan bears lunged into the frothy water and
came up with red and silver fish wiggling in their jaws. The
churning of the stream and the fish jumping drowned out
the sound of bears crashing through the brush and splashing
into the water. It was a cacophony of life and death.

The brother was somewhat stunned as Glen eased the
little skiff toward a small makeshift dock of logs tethered to
shore by a large log ramp that had been flattened off with a
deck hinged onto the float and the shore. Glen tied the skiff
to the dock. Brother Louis could not take his eyes off all the
bears in the stream just thirty yards away, but soon enough
he followed Glen, who was carrying his rifle and the pack
with their lunch in it, up to dry ground.

A narrow path led through the tall grass of the beach
fringe to the woods and another much larger path led to the
cabin site. It was a large cabin with a loft area. The logs were
immense and so well placed that the brother could not see
any gaps in the joinery. The person who had built this home
must have been very proud of his skills with tools.

"It's a beautiful cabin," Glen said as he bounded up onto
the covered porch that sat back in the trees just far enough
to gain protection from the wind, yet still offered a good
view. "I'd give anything to stay here," Glen said as he unslung
the rifle, propped it against the porch railing, and put the
pack on the finely made yellow cedar bench beside the door.
"There is a round in the chamber and the safety is on," he
said, pointing to the rifle, "just so you know."

"Yes . . ." the brother said. "Thank you."

"You been around guns?" Glen asked.

"Not a lot," the brother said. "More since I've lived in
Kentucky. We slaughter our own meat and such. I grew up
in the country and people hunted, but it was in France and

England mostly. There aren't as many guns there. A family might have just one shotgun. It's different here."

"Yeah, we're kinda nuts about 'em. I was raised with 'em."

"I'm glad we have one. Are the bears dangerous?"

"No, not really. They have their minds on eating right now. I suppose if you went right up to them and, you know, tried to wrestle a fish out of their mouth then . . ."

"That might be a problem, yes?"

"Ah . . . yes." Glen smiled at him. He sat down next to his pack and blew his breath on his hands, which were still sore from the fight.

The brother could see the scrapes and the bruising on the knuckles. He paused a moment. "May I ask you something, Glen?"

"Sure, but . . ." and he paused. "I don't know that I'll answer."

"Did I offend you by mentioning my profession when we first met?"

"You mean that thing about loving God?"

"Yes."

"No, Brother, not really. I'm just in bad shape now, I guess. You know how some of 'em that come back from Vietnam will talk about being 'in the shit'?"

"Yes."

"Well, I guess I was in some really bad shit. I know people around here suspect me . . . of things. That I'm different now, maybe into drugs and such." He looked the brother in the eyes. "But it's not true. I'm not a doper now, and I'm damn sure not a burglar. I'm just kinda sad, that's all."

They sat silently. The brother heard gulls in the distance, big animals splashing in the river, and the river itself splashing over rocks. He heard the gentle lowing of a milk cow out in the field. The brother was patient, not wanting to pester the young man to talk.

Glen cleared his throat and started. His eyes were focused on the ground. Sometimes he would stretch his neck back to look into the sky, but never, while he was speaking, did he look at the brother.

"It was March . . . just last spring, around the middle of the month. Or at least I think it was. If there is worse shit to be in, Brother, I really don't want to even imagine it."

"I'm so sorry, Glen."

"Naw . . . not your fault. And I guess it doesn't really have anything to do with God either. I just cannot . . . I mean, absolutely cannot believe that God has any control over what people do to one another. If He did, then . . ." He paused. They both listened to the sound of the stream. Glen's hands trembled and he shook his head. "If He did, then that's just pretty messed up."

Brother Louis shook his own head in silence. "One more question and then let's look around at this beautiful place."

"Sure."

"Do you think if you hadn't been in that war you would still have beaten that man so badly last night?"

Glen smiled bitterly and thought about the question for a moment. "I don't know, Brother. I don't like those two much anyway, and I can't stand the way they even look at Venus."

"Fair enough. Can we build a fire in the cabin, then walk around and come back and eat lunch?"

And that's what they did.

After building a fire in the stove, they walked up by the river and, by way of yelling into the woods, managed to push the bears back into the river or deeper into the tall trees.

There was a trailhead starting just at the mouth of the stream. They hiked up a steep section, which was made of stone and log steps, until they came to a plateau where they could cross to the northwest, away from the creek, and then up to an overlook that offered a good vantage point of the entire homestead.

At the toe of the hill sat the cabin in the trees, then the peninsula, which was covered in long grass now. There was a timber-frame barn with a shake roof and a boat shed next to it, where Glen explained they used to pile hay and feed their cows over the winter. He remembered that Ellie and Slip used to have milk cows for cream and butter at one time. They still had a bull and a cow out on the land and raised a few steers for beef, but they had given up the milking once they started living in town with the rental cabins. Glen explained that the trail went all the way up to the top of the ridge behind them and was a good place to hunt black-tailed deer. It only took an hour or so to get up to the top where you could see all the way down the inlet. When the weather was very clear, a person could see the Fairweather coastal range and the top of Mount Saint Elias, which was the tallest mountain from tidewater in all of North America.

The day had held sunny and the water was still calm. It seemed an idyllic place to the brother. The river itself smelled of rotten fish, but that would only last a few more weeks. The bears, he had to admit, made him nervous. He would have to pray on that—about how he felt living with Alaskan brown bears. Somehow the bears made him think of people's dark animal nature, hunger, and desire. Perhaps this wasn't a bad thing. He wasn't looking for the postcard-perfect setting to commune with God. God was not, after all, meant for just beautiful places.

They walked back down, and Glen showed him the barn. The bull and the cow came and went from the covered water trough. This building, too, showed pride in fine craftsman-ship. Inside there was a workshop and a sawmill built with an old Volkswagen engine, which pushed the saw blade along a track. There were pulleys and ramps, which appeared to be designed to be powered by a workhorse. Out on the point stood two sturdy-looking horses, not much bigger than a child's horse.

Even though it was a near-perfect pastoral scene, serene and beautiful, the brother could not help but feel the weight of whatever Glen was carrying in his heart.

"Those two are Marge and Ole down there. Norwegian

Fjord ponies," Glen said. "Ellie and Slip take care of them and the cows. But Venus mostly comes down here. She loves 'em."

"I can imagine," the brother said, and he thought of the blond girl riding the dignified-looking ponies.

"Is she your girlfriend, Glen?" the brother asked.

Glen grimaced and scuffed at the wet ground braided tightly with the roots of the thick grass. The brother noticed his discomfort and quickly added, "I'm sorry, I don't mean to pry. It's none of my business."

"Naw, that's okay, Brother. It's a fair question." Then he stopped. The old ponies took a few steps toward them, shook their necks, and began feeding again. "There are not many women to choose from here in CS, it's true, but, no, she is just too beautiful, almost angelic, you know?"

The ponies trotted toward them on a well-beaten path. They had on fine leather halters with brass hardware that was turning slightly green.

"And you know, Brother, she is so positive about everything, I feel like I might infect her or something. Pollute her."

"Pollute her?"

"Oh, you know, the things . . . Ah. Never mind. I'm hungry, man. Let's eat."

With that he started walking to the cabin. The brother waited and greeted the Fjord ponies, scratched their ears, hugged their necks, and allowed them to rub up against him. Gulls and eagles circled above the creek where the bears were relentlessly catching and ripping the bodies of already slowly dying fish heading up the river.

Once the brother caught up with Glen the two walked the flats silently. They did not speak to each other. The brother tried to imagine a life here, in this world of falling water, fish, and bears. A coldness seeped into his heart, like loneliness, or a life forever in the shadows.

Glen, as he often did, thought about the war—clouds above calm water and rain shredding up through the trees often made him think of Vietnam. Many of the adult men he knew, men like Slippery Wilson, had served in World War II. These men had endured their own kind of terror, but they also experienced the feeling of belonging to a victorious national movement while Glen never had.

In the old men's war they could look back and see thousands of landing craft and battleships, planes on sorties, tanks churning through the sand up the beach. Their friends fell and they all suffered, yet they died gaining ground toward Paris or Berlin or Tokyo. There was no ground to gain in Glen's war. Glen's war was fought in a haze of boredom and terror punctuated with any numbing drug or sensation they could find: heroin, letters from home, rock and roll, or whiskey and beer. He and a few of his buddies flew out to makeshift towns where men mooched around trying to get high before flying out to the war. There for short periods, they faced death and terror, yet they never gained permanent ground. When the survivors flew back to the little carnival towns they got drunk and fell into nightmarish sleep. It all felt like being desperately alone. It was hard to explain to the old men, or to anyone really, what his war was like.

Louis took in the air: the smell of the fish and the manure, the warm sea-soaked smell of the ponies' hides. Brother Louis closed his eyes at that moment and began running the Jesus prayer silently through his mind: *Lord Jesus Christ, Son of God, have mercy on me, a sinner.* Then he said it over again, but this time slowly and in time with his breath. *Lord Jesus Christ, Son of God, have mercy on me, a sinner.*

One of the ponies gave a great snuffling sneeze and shifted from one foot to the other. He said the prayer again, but this time there were no words, only his breath, and the piercing calls of the birds and the bellows of the ponies.

BACK AT THE cabin they opened all the shutters and even slid open some of the windows, lifting the screens on them, allowing light to fill the front of it. The cabin had warmed enough. Glen was drinking a soda instead of his usual Olympia beer. He unwrapped four sandwiches and had them on plates on the main table in the center of the room. An electric light hung over the table and several other lamps were turned on. The brother pointed at the lights and asked, "How?"

Glen explained that there was a small Pelton wheel generator that ran off water from the stream. There was even a small refrigerator that would hold a couple days' worth of food. Plus, there was an old root cellar in the back of the house. However, there were plenty of problems with the generator depending on the flow from the creek, so there were also a lot of candles and lanterns around.

Glen heated up some water for tea, then sat at the table and ate his meal. Glen didn't speak but simply chewed his food.

Finally, Brother Louis said, "Pollute? I'm trying to think how you could pollute that girl. She obviously is fond of you. I don't think you have done anything to frighten her."

Glen looked at the older man. At first it seemed as if he was going to snap back at Brother Louis, say something about keeping his mouth shut or minding his own business. His eyes under his long hair had that intensity. But then he let out a long breath and just slumped in a kind of acceptance of his fate, as the brother had seen him do at the bar.

"Naw, she likes me, and that's no good."

"Because she is pretty, maybe, technically old enough by law but still too young?"

"Yeah. She just believes everything is so rosy and good. She wants to be a love child."

"And you don't believe in love and goodness?"

"Fuck no." Then he looked up apologetically, and in an outrageous Southern accent said, "Excuse mah French."

The brother smiled at him. "Of course . . . Have you talked to anyone about the impossibly bad shit?"

"I did . . . I talked to the in-country brass. I spilt my guts, Brother. I told everybody who would listen."

"And did it help?"

"No." Glen got up to put more wood in the fire. "What did they do? They didn't move on any court-martials. They didn't even make any arrests. They threatened me and my pilot with dishonorables. They shipped the kid off somewhere far away. Then they said I had done the right thing and took my statement again and sent me home with an honorable discharge and a Bronze Star. I mean, come on. Did they think it would make me happy to keep my mouth shut?"

"Did you do something terrible, Glen? Do you need to give a confession?"

Glen was standing over the brother now with an axe in his hand.

"No . . . Louis, I didn't do nothing wrong. Not. A. Thing. I mean, other than just being over there. I will confess to that, but can you cleanse my memory of what I saw other people do? Can I confess other people's sins?"

"Ah . . . Glen . . ."

"No! The answer is—no you can't! So what's the fucking use?" He walked to the door, opened it, and threw the axe as hard as he could. It tumbled end over end and stuck perfectly into a fat hemlock tree some forty feet from the porch.

Brother Louis went out to sit on the porch bench. He left the door to the cabin open. The warmth from the stove could be felt from the door. He put Glen's sandwich and a fresh soda on the bench next to him. Out in the pasture the two ponies grazed. Three eagles rode a thermal above them, and up the creek they could hear a bear bellowing. Glen sat down and, without any prompting, began telling his story.

"It was March sixteenth. This year. I was the door gunner on an airship, just basically running taxi service out into the Quảng Ngãi area. They called it Pinkville. During the Tet Offensive, an entire enemy battalion just seemed to disappear into this group of little towns. There were fucking mines and booby traps everywhere on the ground. We were getting killed out there in Pinkville. Some thirty guys got bagged up and shipped home in the weeks before, and the brass wanted an end to it. You know how some guys get weird and superstitious? They thought this sergeant, a guy who had kept his guys alive . . . was their good luck charm. Somewhere around the fourteenth the sergeant, who was short on time, steps on a mine in the Pinkville area and is KIA, you know, zipped up."

The brother shook his head.

"Everyone was super uptight. They were talking about wiping out the entire population. The idea of trying to sort through to find the VC and, you know, 'the friendlies,' was wearing pretty fucking thin, Brother, but I didn't know how bad it really was. But on the sixteenth, we started seeing shit from the air we never saw before. Our guys were herding old people and children into huts and then throwing incendiary devices inside. The buildings full of women and children and old people going up in flames.

"My pilot put the ship down. He saw a platoon herding a group of children into a ditch with their weapons. My pilot gets out and talks to the lieutenant who seems to be in charge and a grunt who is along with him. He tells them, 'You don't have to do this. I can take care of these children. I can get them to where they need to go.' The grunt just says the only way to take care of these kids is with a hand grenade. My pilot won't leave, and we load the kids into the chopper and take them back to the firebase. I have no idea what happened to them.

"We went back about two clicks, I don't know, a mile from the spot where we got those kids, and there was another ditch full of bodies. There were some possible combatants in the ditch, adult, or almost adult, young men, but what I remember most was all the children, the infants, the old women and young women holding their babies—killed with American M15s or burned badly from incendiary devices. Even with the rotors and being three hundred feet up, I felt like I could smell the stink. The air smelled of cordite, diesel, and the woodsmoke of burning homes. As we got down to about a hundred feet, the bodies in the ditches seemed to extend out of sight in both directions. The earth was red, Brother. I mean, it was naturally red, but the roads and especially those ditches filled up with blood. Even the farm animals were shot dead, lying on the bloody dirt of their pens. I remember one water buffalo lying on its side lunging, trying to stand up but getting its hind legs entangled in its intestines. The animal was bellowing. Soldiers walked by, not bothering to put it out of its misery.

"Somehow, Brother, I saw a small human arm reach out of the gore along the side of the road. It was a small child's arm, and even though it was covered in blood I could see the child was moving its fingers and its arm from underneath a pile of bodies. I told my pilot to put down, and this time I got out. Without even thinking about it, I waded waist-deep into the bodies. You know, those boots we wear over there are meant to let the water flow in and out. My socks were soaked with blood that night. My pants smelled like rotten meat. I burned them the next day.

"The soldiers from Charlie Company on the ground laughed at me. One offered to shoot the boy once I got him out. He even brandished his fucking sidearm at me, but my copilot shot a round over his head and told me to hurry up and bring the kid. The kid, who was around six years old, was in shock. He wasn't crying or nothing, but his eyes were blinking, and he was breathing hard, but he could still walk and run on his own. I threw a pack of fucking cigarettes at the grunts. I don't know why I threw 'em. I was like, 'Here! Don't kill us,' and we booked it to the chopper."

Glen sat silently for a moment. He started to take a bite of his sandwich, but he stopped, put it down, then took a deep breath.

"I gave a statement to army investigators. They weren't happy about it. I got my papers and I came home."

"What about the boy you rescued? What happened to him?"

Glen paused, and from the look in his eyes, the brother could tell that his guts hurt.

"I have no idea, really. He was turned over to another unit of South Vietnamese who were told to find him a home. He probably went to work in some place in Saigon."

"Is the investigation into all this still going on?" the brother asked.

"I dunno."

"Where did this all happen?"

"Where I picked up the little boy. On the road between two villages that don't exist anymore: My Lai and My Khe."

"Let me ask you an important question just about you, Glen."

"Okay."

"Do you feel responsible for what happened there?"

Glen chewed on his sandwich. The eagles were still circling, and the ponies snuffled in the tall grass, the sound of the stream sizzled in the air. There were no helicopters overhead and no gunfire, no women shrieking nor water buffalo bellowing in agony.

"I could have done more." Tears fell onto his lips as he chewed his food. "I had a big fucking gun on that helicopter."

The brother put his hand on Glen's knee. "You feel terrible, Glen, because you still have a conscience." He cupped the young man's head in his hands and kissed the top of it. "You have not become overwhelmed by numbness. The numbness of materialism or alcoholism or cynicism. You are still a good man, and although it's hard to believe it, your suffering is evidence of your goodness."

"Well, thanks a lot for that." Glen sniffled as the brother let him go from his embrace.

"It's true. If you didn't suffer after seeing such a thing, then I would wonder if you had lost your soul. But you still have a soul, Glen."

Glen started shifting where he sat, suddenly uncomfortable with the intimacy between the two of them.
Uncomfortable with how much he had exposed and how
much more he might expose to this relative stranger. He
suddenly stood up, grabbed onto the brother's arms, and
started wrestling with him as if they were two bears in the
creek. The brother was laughing now. Glen started singing
"Soul Man," which he had learned from one of Venus's Sam
and Dave albums. They fell down laughing in the grass. Glen
was crying now. The ponies trotted over to them to see if they
could gather an idea of what was going on.

One of them, the older one named Ole, put his nose
down and snuffled against Glen's face. He got up laughing
and let the brother go.

"We should get back to town. You wanted to find something in the encyclopedia."

On the way back to Cold Storage the water was still
smooth, but there was a gentle wind on the stern of the little
tin skiff. In the brother's mind, the Jesus prayer still silently
played in time with his breath. He slowed his breathing and
looked at Glen steering the skiff, wondering how in the
world such a young man could ever be healed, wondering
how such a young man could ever rest and trust God in
order to ever feel safe again.

Glen was unusually happy. He felt better after talking with
Brother Louis, and yet in his mind he still saw the red soil of
Vietnam just under the surface of everything before him, as
if it were the pentimento of an original nightmarish reality
bleeding through the lovely setting of his current life.

*Lord Jesus Christ, Son of God, have mercy on me, a sinner.*
*Lord Jesus Christ, Son of God, have mercy on me, a sinner.*

# 6
# I'M A SOUL MAN

When Glen and the brother arrived back at the harbor and began to tie up the skiff, Slippery walked over and helped with the lines. He cleated the skiff off with an old buoy as a bumper and snugged both lines up tight. He asked Glen if the gun was unloaded and Glen jacked the shell out of the chamber, put it in his jacket pocket, then took the magazine out, showed Slip the empty chamber, and handed him the rifle.

Slippery looked down at the brother and spoke softly. "I want to walk you over to our friend George's boat. I think I mentioned to you that George used to be in law enforcement and still serves as a kind of unofficial cop around here. At least he has a lot of friends among the cops. He's got a lot of good stories and he hears a lot of things, a lot of gossip. I think you would want to meet him. He's right down here."

Glen watched Slippery with a bemused look.

"George is no cop. He runs the supply boat. He's got no more authority than you or me."

"I know that, Glen, but he drinks coffee with the right people and keeps up on the news, you know? He has good stories, and if the cops need anything out here, he is the first person they call to help them out."

Glen helped Louis out of the skiff and up onto the float. "George tried to arrest Ellie and Slip back in the thirties for

some labor shenanigans, but he never got it done. He just
followed them out here and decided to stay."

"And he's been keeping an eye on us to this day, but we
haven't broken any laws since."

"I don't know about that." Glen smiled as he shouldered
past them on the narrow harbor float.

"Okay . . . any important laws."

They walked down the finger toward the ramp up to
the boardwalk. Some kids were playing in front of the café,
bouncing a ball around on some squares drawn with chalk.
The girls wore skirts and had their hair in pigtails. The boys
had buzz cuts, sports shirts, and baggy jeans with cuffs tucked
up to their ankles. The clothes looked to be new and stiff, as
if they had just arrived for school. Glen excused himself and
said he was going home for a shower and might have dinner
up at the café around six, which almost sounded like an invitation to the brother's ears, so he smiled and waved goodbye
in a noncommittal way, being almost certain he would see
Glen soon enough.

Slippery and the brother turned at the intersection of
the main finger and went to the largest slip close to town
where the *Phalarope* was moored. The *Phalarope* was an
eighty-foot wooden ship built originally as a US military
patrol boat. She had been built to carry two massive high-
speed engines and tons of fuel, guns, and ammunition to
fight the Japanese. She had a planing hull meant to slide
on top of the water, but now she carried one old Jimmy
engine, half the fuel capacity, a mast, winch, boom, and
lots of space below decks and above for a shore launch or
more supplies to be carried on deck. The *Phalarope* at the
moment was in the business of delivering supplies to the logging camps and the newer small villages up and down this
section of the Pacific Coast. George Hanson, the former
Seattle detective, was the master, scheduler, and cook on
board. His hundred-pound dog, Dot, was the head of security and garbage delivery.

Slippery rapped on the hull. "Hello, the ship!" which set off a good deal of barking. Slip looked at the brother. "George is home. Don't worry about the dog. She is all bluff," and they headed up a set of hanging stairs onto the deck. The big dog came bellowing out fierce and wiggling. Dot was mostly threatening to lick them both and to bury her nose in their crotches. She wiggled her tail, jumped, and pushed them back.

"God damn it, get down now, you hound!" George Hanson came out of the wheelhouse and threw a piece of smoked venison down on the top of the hatch cover, and the dog, who looked something like a Rottweiler and a floppy-eared hound, bounded onto it with both feet, grabbed it with her jaws, and began whipping it back and forth violently.

"Don't grab ahold of it. She'll just want to play tug of war, damn hound . . . Come on in, come on in."

They settled in the main salon of the comfortable ship. George poured himself some tea and by gesture offered it around. The brother accepted and, again from gesture, was told to grab a mug that hung on a hook over the small sink, grab a tea bag from a large tin can on the shelf, and take milk and sugar from the appropriate ceramic bowls. Once settled, George shook hands with the brother and the three men sat at what served as a galley table.

"I been going mostly in a big circle all summer. Here, Sitka, Juneau, and back here. I hit every little spot that needs fuel or bits and bobs along the way. Tomorrow I'm taking a sewing machine and five hundred gallons of diesel fuel down to a gold mine on the outside coast. No trouble since I'll be going by there anyhow. In Sitka I'll pick up orders for Tenakee and a brand-new camp at Corner Bay. Then I'll go to Juneau and pick up more supplies for Gustavus and here. It's like that. I won't get rich, particularly now that that girl Annabelle is flying her big old tractor through the skies and lands anywhere, dropping off thousands of pounds of goods and services at a whim and a thank you, ma'am. Slippery, is

it true she flew a planeload of cold beer and hot pizza up to
Lake Suloia for some loggers just the other day?"

Slippery shook his head, laughing.

George's face was kindly when he said, "Well, by God,
there is no way a man can compete with that—cold beer and
hot pizza, fresh from town, you can't beat that. How'd she
manage that?"

"She flew to Sitka from Corner Bay and told all the boys
over the radio that she had an empty flight coming back
from Sitka and she would make them a good deal if they
wanted a plane full of anything." Slippery was obviously
proud of his niece. "She just figured it would be good adver-
tising to cut them a deal like that."

"Well, good for her. I don't imagine their fire and safety
officer liked it much, but she don't have to keep him happy
right now. Won't be any fires to worry about." George took
a good long sip.

George had blue eyes and was older than the others the
brother had met. George could have been the old Scandi-
navian pastor of the clan: rawboned and earnest, handsome
enough to still turn a woman's head.

"Well, by God," George said, "I was having coffee in
Juneau with some FBI types and your name came up." He
looked at Brother Louis.

"Really?"

"Yep. Now let me get this straight. You go by Brother Louis
back at the abbey in Kentucky, but supposedly in the rest of
the world your name is Thomas Merton?"

"Yes, that's true. I explained that to Ellie."

"Except the part about your real name."

"Well, she didn't seem to want or care to know it."

"Fair enough. Our Ellie isn't all that curious, particularly
about people she likes, and she likes you."

"But it's true. Anyone can talk with my abbot. He gave me
permission to look for a remote place to live where I could
have a quiet life and work on my writing. I could minister to

a small group of people if they were amenable, and I could pray to God and mind my own business."

"Well, these FBI types are not all that happy about you settling down in Alaska. They say you are a Communist sympathizer."

"Well, Mr. Hanson—" the brother started to explain.

"You can call me George."

"George, I'm not sure what the laws are here in Alaska, but I'm a Trappist monk and have devoted my life to loving God. As such, I'm 'sympathetic' to a lot of things, like peace and quiet, books, kindness, and the love of all mankind, and I suppose that might occasionally include police officers, FBI types, and . . . Communists."

George squinted over his tea. "Now I'm sorry to ask you this, Brother, but might it also extend to sympathy toward young women?"

"Oh my," Louis said softly, his face reddened with what could have been embarrassment or rage. "Your friends in the FBI do seem to like their gossip."

"Yes, Brother, they do get around. They mentioned that you may have wanted to leave your posting in Kentucky because of your involvement with a young woman whose name started with an *M*? She was a student?"

"She was a student nurse. I injured my back and she helped me back to health. She was twenty-six years old. Yes, I know that is quite a bit younger than my fifty-two years, but while this relationship has been the subject of my thoughts and prayers, I'm sure the law enforcement community in Kentucky has confirmed that there is nothing in M's and my relationship that concerns them."

"I don't mean to harass you, Brother. I've even had time to read most of your book." George leaned over and, from the seat next to him, picked up a volume with a photo of the brother in robes, *Seven Storey Mountain*. "I like it. I don't find it subversive. I mean, I was looking for something that might indicate that you were pro-Communist, and I didn't see it.

But you know, there are some out there who say I lost my ability to judge. I mean, you didn't serve in the war, Slip and I did. But you were younger and you had a different calling. You grew up in a different world than we did. I see that and I respect that."

"It is true that I did not serve, but I lost my brother during the war. He was a brave man, and I take pride in his service. No one can look at my writing or my record and say that I'm un-American, or anti-military."

"I saw that about your brother in the book, and I'm sorry. I'm not saying you don't love your country or your god. I'm just saying . . . I guess I'm just saying that out here we just have to trust each other. And not coming clean right away with Slip and Ellie that you might want to live at their place while you might be bringing some bad attention out here is something we don't like . . . or need."

"What do you mean 'bad attention'?"

"I guess I've taken the wrong way about this, but . . . this is what I wanted to tell you. One of these FBI guys is going to come out here and take a look at you."

"Really?"

"Yes, sir. He said he is headed out tomorrow. He might go fishing too."

"I will welcome his visit. Now, are you going to be in trouble for telling me?"

"Shit, Brother, I don't work for him and he knows that. He expected me to tell you. He knows Alaska. I half expect he told me to see if you would run."

"That's interesting. What's his name?"

"Mr. Boston Corbett. He's an interesting guy."

"I'm sure he is."


THAT NIGHT BROTHER Louis ate dinner with Glen at the café. He forgot about finding an encyclopedia, but the name Boston Corbett was stuck in his mind like a sliver in a thumb. He arrived early and sat by himself in the corner of the small room adjacent to the kitchen, trying to think how he knew the name. There were two Native women working in the kitchen, one at the grill and the other hustling back and forth from the cooler to the tables to the prep area. The other patrons said nothing to the brother as he came in, but everyone looked at him and gave him a nod and a smile as he walked through and sat down at a two-person table.

A small boy in diapers walked around eating a large cookie. He tottered up and held it out to the brother and said something indecipherable.

"It looks good, but I think I'm going to wait for my dessert. But thank you," the brother said to the little brown-skinned boy with thin hair sticking straight up.

"Bhaaat ahaaat?" the boy said.

"Yes, I agree. It looks good, but I'm going to eat my dinner first."

The woman who was the sous chef and waitress came up and put her hand on top of the boy's head. "What, you don't like our cookies? What's wrong with you?"

The cook was named Deedee. She and her sister, Karen, ran the café. They had grown up in the Tlingit village of Angoon. Their parents had died in a house fire when they were eighteen and twenty. They had taken their inheritance and the insurance money and built the café in Cold Storage eight years before.

Deedee looked rather severely at the brother, then back down at the half-chewed and gummed-up chocolate chip cookie. She laughed, took a napkin off the counter, took the cookie from the child, then asked the cook, "Can you get me a fresh one for Carl?" One of the customers at the counter reached up and took another cookie out of the jar by the register and gave it to the boy before he started bawling.

"And, hey, Janie . . . I think he is muddy. Can you change him?" The young woman by the door waved the boy over and grabbed a diaper bag and took him outside.

"Now . . . that's better. What can we get you today?"

The brother looked her in the eyes and said, "I am easy to please, but I don't know what you serve. Can you recommend something?"

"How hungry are you?"

"Very."

"Do you like fish and chips? We make it with fresh halibut, our own beer batter, real potatoes, and clean oil. That's the secret for good fish and chips . . . good, clean oil and fresh ingredients."

"I believe you. One for me. I'm going to be eating with Glen when he gets here. Could you put his meal on my tab too?"

"That makes two fish and chips. To drink?"

"I'll just have water and whatever Glen wants."

"Okay then, two fish and chips, one water, and two Olys . . . no glass."

"Perfect."

At that moment, Venus and her father walked in. Venus squealed and ran to the back and sat down opposite the brother.

"Oh my gosh," she said softly, "you are a famous writer. That is so cool. I saw your picture in your book. We were all looking at it at the school today. Far out!"

Her father walked up, smiling. He was still wearing his vest and dungarees. The brother wondered just how Mr. Myrtle spent his time when he wasn't playing in a band in Cold Storage.

"Mr. Merton! It's such an honor to meet you," he said quite loudly. "I have so much respect for your work. I'm so sorry I didn't recognize you last night. I wouldn't have been so rude. I was just a little discombobulated."

"Oh . . ." The brother was embarrassed now, and the other patrons looked at him again trying to figure out what the big deal was about this guy. "Oh, really, don't worry at all. There is no reason you should have recognized me. After all, what are the chances that a Trappist monk from Kentucky should just show up here in Cold Storage?"

"Well, word is you are on a world tour to look for a place that you can write in peace."

"See, that's not entirely accurate. I . . ."

Venus was over at the counter ordering a hamburger and a Coke. She was holding hands with Karen, who had taken a moment to say hello.

"So you might be *moving* here!" Venus yelled, then she kissed Karen's cheek and flung herself clumsily back to the table. The little boy came toddling back inside and made a run for the brother.

"I don't know . . . Ah, Venus . . . there is a lot . . ." the brother stammered.

"Hey, Carl!" Venus picked up the toddler. Her father sat down at the table. Venus sniffed Carl's butt, which seemed like a natural thing. "Ooh, clean baby!" Venus said. "The brother is going to move here."

"I really hope you consider it, Mr. Merton. We would love to have you in our community," Mr. Myrtle said.

"Well, I . . . first things first . . ."

"Oh, I understand. You probably have a lot of places to choose from. I understand." Mr. Myrtle held his hands up in front of him as if showing that he was trying to slow his own attack of enthusiasm. "It's just that I have had quite a spiritual journey myself, and I do a little writing . . ."

"Wonderful," the brother said, "but what I really wanted to tell you is I arranged to have dinner tonight with Glen Andre, and I thought you might have some . . . I don't know . . . feelings . . . about Glen being around Venus."

"No, no, no . . . Well, maybe, but I'm sure that's not going to be any problem long term, if you decide to come back . . . to live, that is."

"Ah, well, that's wonderful, but I was thinking more of just tonight. You see, I've already ordered both of our dinners."

"Oh, don't mind that. We are used to such things around here."

Carl held out his now well-gummed second cookie to the brother.

"Bhaaat ahaaat?" Carl said even more loudly than the adults were speaking.

"Yes, Carl, I agree. It is rather confusing," the brother said, smiling at the fuzzy-headed boy being held by the young goddess.

At that moment Glen walked into the café. Venus carried Carl to his mom, who was back at the corner door talking with her friends. Mr. Myrtle was shaking the brother's hand as if it were a bellows.

"Hey, Glennie," Venus said in a cheerful voice, kissed him on the cheek, then said, "Louis is going to move back here after he goes to Asia. George said the people in Juneau knew all about it. Isn't that far out?" Then she was out the door.

"I can't wait to talk to you more about your writing. Perhaps you could come to dinner tomorrow night at our house?" Mr. Myrtle asked.

"Ah . . . certainly," Brother Louis said, without being quite certain what he was agreeing to.

"Very cool. I have some homemade beer and wine. Would you like to try some of that?"

"Ah . . . no, don't go to the trouble."

"No trouble at all!" Then he was out the door, ignoring Glen, and joined his daughter. Venus jumped on his shoulders and kissed her father on the cheek, then walked alongside him. He gave her a side-arm hug, his hand low down in the valley of her hip as they walked away arm in arm. It seemed to the brother that her father had his hand in her back pocket.

"How in the heck does everyone seem to know, or think they know, everything about my life?" Louis asked Glen as the young man sat down at the table, suddenly quiet.

"Thomas Merton?" Glen said.

"Yes, that's my name. But I wasn't using it."

"Because you are a Communist and a peacenik?"

"Peacenik maybe. Certainly not a card-carrying Communist."

The sisters appeared to seamlessly switch jobs, and Karen brought out their meals. "I'm going to have to read your books now," she said as she set down platters of fish and chips. "Is there lots of sex in them?"

"I'm afraid not. I'm sorry."

"That's okay . . . I heard you were some kind of spy." She patted him on the back, turned around to the counter, then grabbed the glass of water and the two beers and set them on the table. "I'll bring you some tartar sauce and ketchup. Anything else?"

"He's not a spy, Karen," Glen said. "He's like a priest but smarter. He writes poetry and biographies and stuff." Glen was already eating the french fries.

"Okay, then . . ." Karen said, already on to her next task and away.

"Really? How do people think they know all this?"

"Welcome to Cold Storage." Glen popped his Olympia beer and sucked the froth that spit up. "The land of no secrets."

"Do they know about the things you told me earlier?" Louis asked as he tried the halibut, then sat back in a kind of wonder at how good it was.

"I don't know. Probably. You are the only one I've told about it since I've been back, though. But, still, they seem to know everything. I thought it was through body language or some kind of mind-meld kind of thing."

"I'm serious, Glen."

"I am too. It mostly works on anything that has to do with sex," Glen said, whispering the word *sex*. "Some of these old women just seem to know." He looked at the cooks. "Those two, I'm telling you, you think about sleeping with someone and these old girls will know about it. It's spooky. One of the reasons I have never, ever, done anything with . . . not even close . . . with Venus."

"Well, they will be disappointed with the gossip I generate," the brother said.

"Come on, it sounds like you have had some things to talk about there, Brother." Glen smiled as he spoke.

"For God's sake, no!" Brother Louis raised his voice. "I told your amateur policeman that I had fallen in love with a student nurse—a woman who is nearly thirty years old now—which was not appropriate with my position at the abbey, and I am still working on my repentance." Louis was now doing the kind of whisper-shrieking that was not at all uncommon in the Cold Storage café.

"Okay, okay . . . calm down. I believe you, and everybody else that I've talked to does too . . ." He ate in silence for a moment. "But that's mostly because everyone assumes that I'm sleeping with Venus."

"Oh Lord, deliver me!" Louis muttered.

"She is crazy about me, Brother. I can't help that. She thinks it's so romantic that I went off to war. She wants out of this town so bad. She wants to see the world, and she has all these ideas about Paris and revolution and living in an artist's commune."

"You say that Venus wants to leave Cold Storage?" the brother asked.

"That's the way she talks with me. She acts like she can't wait to get away from her parents. Apparently, the subject of her going to college is squelched every time it comes up. Mom and dad say there isn't enough money, and Venus was born to stay around Cold Storage—she is really good on a boat. She could fish with anyone. Hell, she could run a fishing boat of her own. I think that's what Bobby and Esther want for Venus."

The brother was now eating the fish and chips with more enthusiasm than he was expecting. He drank a long draft of the cold water and thought about Glen and Venus. Glen was much too damaged and Venus was much too open for them to be even small-time crooks. He couldn't picture either of them breaking into houses.

Karen was taking another order and had her back toward Glen and the brother. "Do you think that Venus might be stealing stuff around town?" The brother looked at Glen, and the damaged young man seemed to flinch, then look out the window.

"Naw," was all he said. Then, after thinking, he asked, "Why are you worried about that?"

"I think Venus is a complicated soul. I hate to think of her . . . I don't know . . . going toward the bad and ruining her life."

"I don't think you have to worry about that, Brother." Glen finished his first beer and belched softly.

"Well, I might as well ask the oracle," the brother said much more loudly than he had intended. He reached over and tugged on the co-owner's sleeve.

She spun and smiled at him.

"Karen, I can tell you are a good friend to Venus—she appears to be fond of you—but here is one question I've been thinking about," Brother Louis said to the sometimes–sous chef. "Do you know who has been stealing things from your business and other people's houses in the last few months?"

The Tlingit woman dropped her smile. She appeared to be looking back into her memory or perhaps into her consciousness then pulled up a rickety chair and sat down. "I try to be a good friend to Venus, Brother. I try to be a good friend to everyone in this town. That means I don't speculate on things like that." She stood up and wrung her hands on the table rag. "Let me get you two some rhubarb crisp and a cup of coffee."

"Perfect," Louis said.

"You are going to be able to drink coffee? 'Cause you probably won't sleep much tonight with that cop flying in to see you tomorrow."

"Oh my Lord, Karen!" the brother said, and she chuckled, then continued at some kind of right angle.

"But I will tell you what: that girl is a lot tougher than anyone knows." She paused again, scanning her thoughts for a moment, and then said, "Way tougher."

Just then, out on the boardwalk, a squall of noise seemed to be moving up from the dock and around the corner. Children started running past the café. Some were holding sticks, some held colorful wands, which appeared as though they had been decorated by the kids themselves. The brother began to recognize the sound as music.

Karen looked at both men. "My gracious. It sounds like Wilber is drinking again."

"Uh-huh," Glen said before taking another drink of his own beer.

Wilber Whitman was a man who had tied a large battery-operated tape player to the front of his bicycle, and when he reached a certain sweet spot of inebriation, he would ride up and down the boardwalk playing a tape of old carousel music at top volume. The bike veered from handrail to handrail, and the children cheered him on, waving colorful paper in the air. When this happened during the day, the loud music prompted an impromptu parade: kids, sometimes wearing newspaper hats, waving colorful sticks—sometimes wrapped in tape or paper—marching or dancing to the churning mechanical sound of a merry-go-round: sticks on loose drumheads, cowbells, wheezing calliope-like pipe organs, and bent cymbals banging together.

Ravens and eagles, which you might think would fly off at the first hint of the racket, would often just fly up to the roofline of the nearby houses to watch the spectacle from there.

After the procession passed by the café twice and disappeared in the distance, Venus came inside holding young Clive by the hand. Clive had a runny nose and was carrying an old balloon stick with ribbons wrapped around it. The deflated balloon hanging from it had shrunk to the size of a weathered orange.

Venus and the child sat perched at the counter and Venus asked for milk and a cookie for Clive. When she twirled around on the stool, she stopped and stared at Glen and the brother.

"You guys still here?"

"Of course," the brother said. "What else are we going to do?"

"Are you kidding?" Venus said, looking genuinely puzzled at them both. "There is so much to do. Clive and I were chasing crabs since we saw you, and we've been in a parade! Now we are going to share a cookie, eat my leftover burger, then we are going to dance and listen to records in my room. I just don't know if I have time to do everything I've got planned." There was just a hint of sarcasm in Venus's voice, a little pepper there that lent truth to what Karen had disclosed.

"Who is your favorite band right now?" the bother asked.

"I LOVE the Beatles. Love, Love, Love!" She was spinning on the stool and trying to flip her blond hair off of her dirty face.

"Me too," he said. "Who is your favorite?"

"I LOVE THEM ALL FOR DIFFERENT REASONS!" Her voice was rising in pitch and volume.

"Love, love, love," mumbled three-year-old Clive as he grabbed for the cookie that Karen gave him.

"Paul is the cutest, George is the most serious, Ringo is the most fun, and John is the most creative . . . He is also married." Venus got down off her stool and balanced Clive, who was eating his cookie, at the counter as Karen got up from the table and watched the small boy. Venus walked over to Glen and plopped down into his lap.

"I think Glennie looks like George. He even walks like George, stiff-legged like a cowboy," she said, and then curled up close like a little girl wanting to be read a story. But she was not a little girl. Now Glen was uncomfortable.

"Jeez, V," Glen said and squirmed out from underneath

her, pushing her onto the chair Karen had vacated. She seemed a little bit embarrassed as she gathered herself together, running her fingers through her hair, then sitting up straight.

"Venus, should I bring something to your house for dinner tomorrow?" the brother asked.

"Do you have any records or candles or a guitar?"

Brother Louis laughed softly and smiled at the girl, who more and more reminded him of a type of forest nymph imagined by Shakespeare.

"No, dear, I don't have any of those things."

"Oh . . . that's okay then."

THE NEXT MORNING Brother Louis decided to write in his journal and pray. He also met Mr. Myrtle at the schoolhouse where he looked up some very useful information in both a high school history book and the *Encyclopaedia Britannica*. He then ate a very light breakfast at Ellie's Bar and drank coffee with fresh milk. He had decided that he would wait for the FBI agent with a clear mind and an open heart.

He read scriptures all morning, reading most of Romans and paying particular attention to 12:9–14, which speaks of genuine love for those who seek to persecute you. *Let love be genuine; hate what is evil, hold fast to what is good, love one another with brotherly affection, outdo one another with showing honor.* He was clearheaded and unafraid by the time he heard the floatplane circle the town and land near the harbor around noon. He got up and started to walk toward the harbor because he had decided to save Agent Corbett the trouble of looking for him.

As he made his way down toward the ramp, the fat old man was once again sitting out by his front door eating raw clams. He looked up and nodded at the brother.

"'Lo," he said.

"Hello, sir. How are the clams today?"

"Same as they were yesterday. Perfect."

"Good to hear. I'm glad you are enjoying them."

"Hey . . ." the old man said.

"Yes, sir?" the brother answered and stopped walking.

"My pop told me never to talk to the cops without a lawyer."

"Your father was a wise man. Do you have any lawyers in town?"

"Hell no," he said. He then slurped down another clam and threw the shell down onto the pile under his house.

"Well . . . I guess I'm out of luck." The brother waved.

"You could take this." The old man leaned over in his chair and picked up a short smoothed-off piece of wood, which could only be a fish club. "Whack him across the snout if he gets sassy."

The brother looked at the old man a moment to consider if he was teasing or not. The old man laughed and wiped his face with his handkerchief.

"That's what we do to the old men in brown coats, or at least that's what my grandpa said he did."

"Well, thanks for the advice. I'll come get it if I have to."

"Goodbye then, Mr. Brother."

"Yes, sir. What is your name by the way?"

"I'm Grandpa Joe. Don't let him take you to jail, Mr. Brother Louis."

"I won't, Grandpa. I'll tell him to talk with you."

"Oh no! I want nothing to do with the cops. You know, they come out here and mess around and don't do nothing. You know, some of these punks around here came into my house and creepy-crawled around while I ran up town."

"Did they take anything?" The brother stretched and leaned against the rickety table near the door of Grandpa Joe's cabin.

"Just a canning jar full of coins. You know, not a lot of money and nothing valuable. More that they were just in here."

The old man ate another clam. The brother just watched.

"They took a book too. Crazy, 'cause one of my grand-daughters went down to California and ended up working on some hippie place in the mountains, somewhere near Sacramento. This guy she worked for wrote a book about building trails for the Forest Service. She sent it to me. I used to build trails around here. I guess she thought I would like it, and damn it, that book is missing. It was a bunch of poems. I never even read the thing."

"Do you remember the title?" the brother asked.

"Sure. It was called *Riprap*. I remember that because my father taught me how to stack rocks on the side of a trail on a steep part, build a little wall, and then backfill from the uphill side to make a trail on a slope. *Riprap*. You don't use mortar or anything, just pile the rocks the right way. I used to love to stack rocks when I was younger."

"I know that book," the brother said. "Your granddaughter is lucky."

"Well, I don't know about that. She gave me my first great-grandchild." Grandpa Joe sucked down another clam, then added one more clam to a quart jar of others. "Well, don't give the coppers nothing." He waved his paring knife in the air as a way to indicate their visit was over.

"I will give unto Caesar," the brother said, and he started to walk away.

"But not too much," Grandpa Joe blurted out.

They both laughed, waved some more, then parted company.

AGENT CORBETT, IT turned out, was from Louisville. He was dressed straight out of an L.L. Bean catalog. Even Brother Louis thought he looked like he was dressed for a walk to take in the fall colors in Maine instead of a trip to an Alaskan bush community, although the Bean boots were popular at the time in the forty-ninth state. Corbett had a flattop haircut and had lit up his Camel cigarette the moment he got off the plane. He had something of a

GI demeanor about him, particularly in how he spat in his palm, quashed his cigarette butt right there in the puddle of spit, then tore up whatever was left and scattered it on the ground. He wasted very little of his tobacco, and he seemed keenly aware of both fire hazards and the impact of trash or trace evidence he left behind.

The agent liked the feel of this Alaskan town: cool and fresh. He was growing weary of his life in the South. Steamy summers that felt as though every place you went someone was running a hot bath. Sweat-soaked shirts and dresses. Sweat on your forehead and neck. Here the air was cool all over, and it made him think more quickly, so much so that he craved a cold glass of whiskey simply to slow his troubling thoughts.

He was hoping to solve a big problem by coming out here. His boss hated the writer, this friar or whatever the heck he was. His boss was convinced the writer was a flat-out Communist spy. Boston Corbett didn't particularly care if he was or not, but the friar gave Boston a reason to fly across the country and all the way out here to solve the big problem he had. He didn't like the thought of what he might have to do. He was hoping he wasn't going to have to kill someone to solve his particular problem, but it had grown into such a mess he was ready to do just that if he had to.

The strong-looking man who walked with a confident manner down the dock was Thomas Merton. Boston Corbett could recognize him from the surveillance photos in his file. They shook hands briefly and made introductions. The brother suggested they talk up at the bar or the café. He said that Ellie's Bar would be much more private this time of day. If they really needed to, they could go to his cabin. The agent looked him over as if trying to assess how much danger there would be either way, and the brother could see that he could barely resist frisking him right there.

"No, Agent Corbett, I am not armed. I actually had to ask for an armed escort to go out to the cabin I was looking at yesterday . . . armed because of the brown bears in the river."

"Do you own a gun, Brother?"

"No, sir. I suppose you do . . ."

"A few."

"Then we should be safe from the bears."

ONCE THEY WERE settled on going to Ellie's Bar, they sat in the corner. Glen was there of course, eating a sandwich and drinking an Olympia. Ellie's bans on drinking in her establishment never lasted long. Glen put on "Are You Experienced?" by The Jimi Hendrix Experience, which seemed to irritate the agent a bit, but he didn't ask him to turn it off.

"Now, Mr. Merton. I'm sure George Hanson talked to you about my coming around."

"Yes, sir."

"Small towns being what they are."

"Yes, sir."

"I just want to talk with you about your plans for a few minutes. You are not under arrest or anything like that."

"All right." The brother smiled at the FBI agent congenially. "I suppose you already spoke with my abbot at Gethsemane, so you know my official itinerary that I filed with the State Department?"

"Of course. I have it right here. I'm more interested in the kind of people you plan on speaking with."

"Well, in California, it's mostly religious scholars and Catholic writers. In northern California I imagine I will be meeting with some poets—Mr. Ginsberg hopefully, perhaps Mr. Kesey, or Kerouac, though they are notoriously hard to pin down and my schedule will be tight."

"What kinds of matters will you discuss with these writers?"

"I'm primarily interested in their knowledge and interest in Eastern spirituality, how they pray, that kind of thing."

"Will you be talking about planning peace rallies or demonstrations, 'be-ins,' anything involving praying on the sites of military installations?"

The brother's stomach tightened up. He had guessed that

Agent Corbett might have spoken to the abbot; but the certain knowledge that they had met gave Louis a burning sense of dread.

"No, I don't imagine I will. I don't have time for such things on this trip."

"What else do you want to tell me?"

The brother paused and knew he should consider his answers carefully, but the dread had ahold of him now, and calculation would only seem like lying.

"I'm looking forward to meeting religious leaders in India, including the Dalai Lama, who is in exile from his home in Tibet, and, no, I am not taking him any goods or financial support from any Western supporters. Again, I look forward to speaking with him about his spiritual practices and about his convictions concerning peace and compassion."

"Do you support his appeasement toward the government of Red China?"

"I would hardly call his attitude one of support or appeasement. His Holiness is a man of profound religious faith who has given up his position to save the lives of hundreds of thousands of his countrymen. He sat with Mao Zedong and had the chairman tell him that his religious faith and all of his sacrifice was nothing but 'pornography,' and yet he stays committed to a peaceful resolution to an intractable conflict. Such is his faith that he prays for the seemingly impossible."

The brother's voice was gaining a harder tone of anger or perhaps desperation, but he did not stop smiling, and he did not take his eyes from the agent's eyes.

"Agent Corbett, would you mind if I ask you two questions of my own that have got me wondering?"

"Of course," the agent said as he leaned back and lit another cigarette. Ellie brought an ashtray and two glasses of water over to their corner table. "I will answer them if I can."

"Let me know if you boys want something to eat or drink over here," Ellie said, then waved at the table and walked away.

"Am I really the only reason you came all the way out here?"

"Well, that, and to visit with George Hanson and maybe do some fishing." The first puff of smoke from the fresh cigarette whorled around his head. The brother remembered his years of smoking and enjoyed that first pull. "What else you want to know?"

"Is Boston Corbett your real name? I don't think it is."

"Really . . . now, why is that?"

"I'm just of a suspicious nature. You mind showing me your ID?"

The FBI agent smiled and grimaced with his Camel pinched in the corner of his mouth as he pulled a shield and some stodgy ID with a photo from his woodcutter's jacket.

"Now, why the shakedown on my name?" Corbett asked.

"Okay . . ." the brother said, "if that is your real name, then I think your first answer was a lie. You didn't come all the way out here to check on my itinerary, because you already have it. You know I'm going to Thailand to speak at a conference of Catholic scholars. I will give a talk about the Eastern styles of prayer and faith. I will give a quick mention that Catholic monasticism is a communal life much like the Marxist ideal, but is different in that it is clearly centered around faith in God, which is the 'pornography' that Chairman Mao speaks of. So, while I may scare some politicians as being sympathetic to Communism, I'm certain you know that I am clearly not a Communist. You know that in Japan I am planning to meet with Gary Snyder and Philip Whalen, who are both practicing Zen Buddhists. They may be upsetting to the status quo, but they are also not Communists. So, I think you are out here for something else."

"And what would that be? And what about my name made you suspicious?" The agent drank from his glass of water as if his mouth was suddenly cataclysmically dry.

The brother was still smiling as the FBI agent took two more long swallows of his water.

"In 1865, ten days after President Lincoln was shot at Ford's Theatre, a Union soldier named Boston Corbett is said to have shot and killed the assassin John Wilkes Booth in a tobacco shed in Virginia as the shed was set alight by Union troops. It was either a lucky or an extremely skillful shot taken between the widely spaced planks of the walls, which were built to allow tobacco to dry. It was said he shot the wounded assassin right through the skull."

"Wasn't just said, it's the God's truth!" The FBI agent showed more defensive anger in his voice than pride. "That was my grandfather, and I was named for him."

"All right . . . okay . . ." the brother said, "then why do we have two men staying at the same little spot in Alaska, for Pete's sake, from the Deep South, who claim to be named George Atzerodt and Edman Spangler?"

Boston Corbett swung around in his chair and waved to have Ellie come over. He ordered steak and eggs, more water and coffee. He offered to buy Brother Louis anything he wanted to eat, and since the FBI was buying, the brother ordered a piece of huckleberry pie with ice cream and some coffee as well. As Ellie walked away, Agent Corbett lowered his voice and hunched over the table.

"Do you know where those two men are right now?"

"I think they are out fishing for salmon."

"Okay . . . so they are not gonna waltz in here any second while we are talking?"

"No, sir. Not unless something has changed that I don't know about."

"Okay . . . then what do you know about them?"

"Agent Corbett, you must know what I know, and the *Encyclopaedia Britannica* confirms that Edman Spangler was one of the Lincoln conspirators. That in 1865 he was posing as a stagehand at Ford's Theatre. Spangler helped him on the horse, even though Booth's left ankle was broken from the jump from the president's theater box to the stage, and helped him out of town before authorities arrived."

"And Atzerodt?"

"George Atzerodt was part of the plot to kill the vice president. He went to the hotel where the VP was staying, but Atz lost his nerve and got drunk instead. Even though he did nothing but run his mouth and get drunk, George Atzerodt was hung with the other martyrs to the lost cause of the War of Northern Aggression. They want to buy Mrs. Ellie Hobbes's beat-up old mummy."

"Do you know why?"

Ellie brought the coffee, cream, and silverware over.

"Thank you, Ellie," the brother said, looking up at her with kindness in his eyes. She didn't look at the cop and walked briskly back to the kitchen.

"Well, first, I don't think they are old enough to be who they say they are, unless . . . and this may well be after having met you . . . there is some cosmic gathering of relations involved in the Lincoln assassination happening that I had not heard about in the news. And second, I think they believe the mummy stored out in the root cellar of this very establishment is the mummified corpse of John Wilkes Booth."

# 7
# SHE'S MINE

"Okay, let me explain something real quick." Agent Corbett leaned forward, still whispering at this point. "This Booth business is kind of a hobby of mine. My wife says it's an obsession. Let's just say it is. I got wind of these guys hunting around for the Booth mummy while working on the King case. You know, it's a huge case that has a virtually unlimited budget. So my boss said the King case would cover my travel expenses but only if there were other cases I could work on while I was out here."

Agent Corbett trying to explain his travel expenses seemed like what the old farmers in Kentucky would call "a line of bullshit as tall as it was wide," but the brother let it go.

Agent Corbett went on. "They don't think these clowns have a connection to the King assassination, but I turned up your name . . . and my boss in the Louisville office . . . I don't know for what reason . . . he hates you, Brother. He has files all the way back to the army intel and Foreign Services, MI5, CIA. My Lord, he thinks you were in Khrushchev's back pocket all the way back in the fifties."

Corbett slipped his case up to his lap, then took out a sheaf of papers. On the front was a typed label with a long numeric file code followed by the word *speeches*. The brother leafed through the pages without reading carefully. All of the names of Soviet citizens were circled in red ink. The former premier's name was both circled and underlined.

"All I was saying in these remarks was that Khrushchev was a complex figure—enemy of Stalin, an advocate of independent Ukrainian agriculture, brusque, anti-intellectual, sometimes clearly a thug but also flexible and almost anti-Communist at times."

*Jesus Christ*, Boston Corbett thought to himself, *maybe I should go ahead and just put a bullet in this guy's brain.* Like Khrushchev himself, the FBI agent had an intolerance for intellectual gibberish.

The brother leaned back, shook his head, pointed to the agent's cigarettes, and Corbett handed him the pack.

"Really?" the agent said and lit the brother's smoke with a wooden match by striking it on the bottom of the table.

The dread in the brother's stomach somehow made the cigarette taste better.

Corbett said, "All that may be true, but as soon as I mentioned that you were headed to Alaska, they cut me a ticket right then and there."

"My Lord in heaven," Brother Louis said.

"Now, to tell you the truth, Mr. Merton, I'm going to write up my report. I will take some photos of you walking around here. I will take some photos of your writing and stuff. My boss will wet his pants over that. But what I really want to do is figure out what these old boys are doing up here. What the story is with this damn mummy, and what they are really up to with wanting to buy it. But if you mess with me, if you start cutting any fine distinctions, I will be changing your travel plans. You will be traveling with me in cuffs. Does that sound fair?"

"I suppose it depends on the finer details of what you mean by 'mess with'?"

"Don't start with me," the agent said.

The brother looked at the lit cigarette in his hand. Seeing it between his fingers almost shocked him. He felt the dreamy buzz of nicotine in his brain and remembered the pleasant mornings of cigarettes and coffee. But then he remembered the commitment to health he had given M, and he snubbed it out. He drank some coffee then ate a bite of pie, thinking about his activities in Kentucky, which could have possibly drawn the attention of the FBI.

"You say these men, who are here fishing, might be involved in the King assassination?"

Agent Corbett was enjoying his steak and eggs and he ate quickly, talking between bites. "Naw . . . probably not, but you remember that Dr. King was shot on the balcony of that motel in Memphis? Well, this shit bird, James Earl Ray, who can barely read or write, had broken out of prison in Arkansas, makes it down to Memphis, buys a gun, pays up more than a week in a rooming house, which gives him a perch overlooking that balcony. He shoots the minister, makes it out of town, makes it out of the state, makes it out of the God-blessed country to Canada, and buys a ticket to Rhodesia, for poop sake. This dumb cracker can't spell Rhodesia let alone know it is a white separatist homeland. His prints are found all over the rifle and the perch in the boardinghouse bathroom. He gets arrested in London, where he 'confesses' to everything, and then, when he is brought back to the United States, he recants everything and tells the cops he is the 'patsy,' just like Lee Harvey Oswald."

"So . . ." The brother spooned up red huckleberries into the last of his vanilla ice cream.

"So patsy or not, Mr. James Earl Ray had some help. At least with his trip. Buying the gun, getting it sighted in, getting a passport."

"And you think our guests here may have helped him?"

"Have you spoken to them?"

"Yes."

"For longer than five minutes . . . and did the subject of race relations come up?"

"Yes, sir."

"So they are not being too quiet about their beliefs?"

"I would say not," the brother said quietly.

"Gosh darn it!" The agent blew out a long plume of smoke. "You see, Brother, I have listened to hours of taped conversations. I would say they are true believers. I would say they might have put Jefferson Davis to shame."

"Do you have any hard proof of them helping your . . . um . . . shooter?"

"Not really. They have been on this 'hunt' for Mr. Booth since March. They have been hard to locate. Truthfully, I don't know much, but they are suspicious types, and I'm mostly pissed off about this claim that they've got about Booth. It brings dishonor to my family."

"It can't be true, can it . . . that this old mummy would be Booth?"

"The rumor followed his death from day one. My grandfather took the body back to the DC Armory. The federal government had him identified. Remember, he was a famous actor, so it wasn't hard to ID him. But they were not going to allow his dead body to be used to make him a cult hero for the rebels. The doctors examined him, even took some samples, but then it was said the army surgeons dumped his body in the Potomac River. But the lore of the lost cause had it that there were three men in the tobacco shed. Booth survived. My grandfather shot another conspirator, who was identified wrongly as Booth, then Booth crossed into the South, met with the president of the Confederacy, and arranged passage to Europe through New Orleans. In 1914, a man in the Oklahoma Territories, who bore a resemblance to Booth and was known for drinking and reciting long passages of Shakespeare, was holed up in the small town of Enid. On his deathbed, he is said to have told the woman attending him that he was in fact the killer of the Great Emancipator. It's a long story, Brother, but the proprietor of the hotel where he died had him embalmed and charged money for people to see him. Over the years the mummy changed hands and was exhibited in carnivals and sideshows all over the West."

"When was the mummy of Booth last officially seen?" the brother asked as he set aside his empty pie plate.

"Hey, wait a minute. I'm not saying it *is* Booth. I don't think it is. I'm saying that this mummy of an old drunk who could recite a lot of Shakespeare, who said he was Booth, may have been seen in 1920 and was said to have been lost in a train wreck," Agent Corbett said.

Now the brother was confused, and the dread in his gut seemed to increase. The agent was clearly lying about the facts of the King assassination, but he had the strength of personal conviction when discussing this John Wilkes Booth wrinkle. This man might be shoveling a load of shit, but there might be a pony in there somewhere.

"Ellie told us that her father said he had bought the mummy from a man who wanted an old sheepherder wagon her father had, and that the man claimed to have bought the mummy from a railroad baggage-claim auction."

"Did he say when?"

"She didn't mention the date, but from everything else it sounds as if it was after 1914 and after the First World War, and I will say the Southern gentlemen seemed very interested in this little bit of information."

"I can imagine they were."

"How does any of this tie in with Reverend King's murder?"

"You mean other than my travel expenses?"

"Of course."

"These old boys are true believers. I think they want to build a kind of little kingdom that worships the Confederacy. It's just not enough to go out on weekends and re-create battles. They want monuments, not just to what happened but to the spirit of the sacrifice. To murder Lincoln shows that spirit. In some of their recorded conversations they talk about the Lincoln assassination in that way, as if it were a sacred event, and we recorded these conversations just days before the King assassination in Memphis. The Lincoln conspirators were certain their acts would save the rebellion, and the men who killed King believed that they would foment a new one. They were parallel acts of passion and conviction . . . I'm convinced of it." Agent Corbett set aside his empty plate. "That's beyond my family name or my travel expenses."

"What do you want from me, then?" the brother asked.

"Just report to me. Tell me everything they say . . . and get me an invitation to dinner with them, maybe introduce me, and let me interview you to cover the case for my boss."

"Introduce you as what—an FBI agent from Louisville?"

"Sure, I doubt you are much good at lying. Just tell the truth. They don't know me from Adam." Agent Corbett's voice dropped, and he looked down and to the left.

The brother still suspected the agent was lying. But why? If he knew them, he wouldn't need an introduction, unless he didn't want anyone to know that he and the Lincoln conspirators were acquainted.

The agent did some fancy business blowing circles of smoke, then he leaned across the table with his cigarette in his mouth. "Don't mention anything about the Lincoln assassination or that you suspect they are traveling under false names. We'll just see how it goes. I've already got it set up to go fishing with them tomorrow."

Agent Corbett looked around for Ellie and got up to pay the bill.

"Why do you need me to introduce you then, if you already have an appointment to go fishing?" the brother asked.

"I need you on my side. You know them, and I'm sure they run their mouths too. I'm betting they are intrigued with you. These redneck history buffs always want to impress genuine intellectuals, and it's best for me to have a friend of sorts to make the introductions. You know, it's always better to meet men like this once you have a couple of drinks inside you."

"That won't be hard with these two. Are you still going

to check me out?" The brother stayed slouched in his chair, now wishing he had eaten something more substantial.

"Of course I'm checking you out!" Boston Corbett, or whatever his real name was, said. Then, as he walked over to the corner where Glen and Venus were standing, talking on either side of the soda bar, he turned and said over his shoulder, "And if you don't help me out, I'll just take you back to Louisville and give you to my boss for his birthday."

Venus, having heard Corbett's last comment, said, "Oooh . . . checking you out! The FBI agent is checking out my new boyfriend."

"Please don't say that, Venus." The brother's cheeks turned red, and he started making parallel lines in the smears on his plate. "You know that's not true."

She spun around on the stool, then flopped her upper body on top of the counter, flipping her golden hair out across Glen's forearm.

"I KNOW it's not true. Glen is my boyfriend, and I'm going to ask him to dinner tonight too. My poppa said I could."

"That's right"—the brother looked up at Agent Corbett suddenly as he remembered dinner—"I have an engagement tonight. I'm not going to be at Ellie's for dinner. Why don't we meet back here for a drink at five? The fishermen will be back and you can meet . . . Slippery, the boat captain. You can confirm your fishing trip with him."

"Thank you, that sounds good." Corbett looked at everyone and stared a little longer at Venus as she flipped her hair back and spun once again on the stool. He introduced himself to Glen, then turned to speak to the brother again. "So, five at the bar? I can see the two of you gentlemen have some things to work out about this boyfriend situation, so I'll leave you to it."

It bothered Brother Louis much more than it should have that Agent Corbett wasn't smiling as he turned toward Venus and Glen.

"Which of you knows who is doing those break-ins around town?"

Both Venus and Glen leaned back with genuine shock on their faces and Venus stammered, "We don't know nothing about that, and you got a lot of nerve talking to us that way!"

Glen actually laughed out loud at Venus's reaction. The federal agent turned away from them and walked out the door.

# 8

# THE MEAL AND THE ABSENCE OF GOD

At about six o'clock that night, Brother Louis, after getting good directions from Ellie, took a bottle of her
salmonberry cordial as a gift and stood at the front door of a
small cottage at the north end of the boardwalk. The cottage
was built up on the water side on a steep ledge over the water.
He could hear the water lapping on the rocks just below
the house, yet the cottage was surrounded by ancient trees,
nestled in among them like a kitten sleeping at a giant's feet.
The trees must have been more than six hundred years old,
with trunks that seemed far too big for two people to put
their joined arms around.

Introducing the agent to the Southern gentlemen
had been simple enough. They had once again gathered
around the woodstove with glasses, ice, and a fresh bottle
of bourbon. The brother had joined them in a drink earlier
and explained that he and Glen had been invited to someone's house in the community for dinner. The gentlemen
did not inquire, but the brother suspected that they already
knew. When Boston Corbett walked in, Brother Louis was
impressed because he was dressed almost exactly like one of
the gentlemen, in a thick linen shirt with a cashmere sweater
that fit perfectly over his athletic frame and just covered the
leather belt on his pleated cotton pants. His Southern accent
was more pronounced than the brother had remembered
from their meeting earlier.

The only hitch in the introduction was when Mr. Spangler noticed and repeated the agent's name. "Boston Corbett, you say? Well, isn't that something for an FBI agent from Louisville?"

Everyone agreed and let the name slip on by. When Mr. Atzerodt asked what had brought him to Alaska, Agent Corbett said, "Oh, I came up here to talk with Brother Louis." His tone was light as a feather, as if there was not a reason in the world to be concerned. The men laughed as if he'd made a joke.

"The good Brother been robbing some banks, has he?"

"Not at all." Corbett smiled broadly, put his hand on the brother's shoulder firmly, and said, "Not at all. You know these Catholics can't keep their hands off the ladies' bake sale money . . . No, mostly I was just looking for an excuse to come fishing."

Then they were off and running, talking about fishing in Alaska, fishing in the South, and the quality of the bourbon. It was as if their shared affinity was their superiority and their entitlement to the good things at this time of their lives. The brother excused himself and got up, thinking that he would give them some more room in case they wanted to ridicule Northerners or talk about the virtues of public hangings.

HE KNOCKED ON the door of the Myrtles' cabin and heard footsteps bounding down steps inside. The door swung open to a steamy atmosphere of frying meat, boiling tomato sauce, and marijuana smoke. Glen and Bobby Myrtle were standing at a narrow back door smoking a joint. Venus had opened the door wearing painters' coveralls with nothing on underneath. An older woman with long amber hair was adding cooked meat to the tomato sauce. She shrieked, "Venus, you go upstairs right this second and put on some decent clothes. We have company!"

"Sorry," the girl said and bounded back up the steep ladder, where the brother could hear the Beatles playing.

"Hello, Brother Merton." The woman came around the counter of her small kitchen. "Just take your shoes off here." She pointed to a big wooden box of boots. "I'm Esther. I'm Venus's mom, and I'm so happy you could come to dinner. I have to say, Brother Merton, that I love your poetry." She pulled strands of hair off her face, revealing a smudge of tomato paste on her cheek.

"Thank you for inviting me. You don't have to call me Brother. Please just call me Louis, or Thomas, if you like."

"Of course." She was blushing now. The brother knew she wanted to say something more about his poetry, and he wanted to avoid it. *Maybe later,* he thought.

"Would you like a glass of wine? Dinner will be ready soon," Mrs. Myrtle said, making a swaying motion toward an unusually shaped wine jug. The motion was mirrored by her hair and the sway of her long Polynesian-like dress. He declined the wine and handed Ellie's cordial to Mrs. Myrtle and explained it.

"Fantastic," she said. "Ellie makes great-tasting booze."

"Want some pot?" Bobby called from the back door, which was just beyond a small bathroom and a door to what looked like a bedroom.

"No. No, thank you," the brother said, maybe a little more loudly than he intended. Maybe he was thinking that Agent Corbett would be able to hear him decline the marijuana.

"Here, sit." Bobby flopped down on the strange-looking couch that had a hard rolled-up cushion on a frame. "How'd it go with the cops?"

Bobby's hair was wet as if he were just out of the shower. He was wearing what seemed to the brother like uncomfortably short shorts.

"I hope you like garlic!" Esther was yelling over the top of the water that was boiling up, getting ready for the noodles. She had the joint tightly pinched in her lips now.

Bobby flipped a strand of his wet hair off his face and said, "Man, talking to the cops can be such a drag." His eyes were closed now. "Like that time we came back to San Diego from Mexico. God!" Then he sat there on the couch not saying anything, just staring out into space as if he were playing the film of the entire episode on the back of his skull.

Brother Louis walked over to the kitchen and said to Esther, "On second thought, I would like a little bit of wine." Then he walked back near the stove and sat on a nicely made pile of firewood. He looked up at Glen, who was not speaking but smiling to himself, silently nodding to the rhythm of the Beatles' "Love Me Do" coming from upstairs.

As no one was speaking, Brother Louis cleared his throat and said, "Actually, the conversation went really well," and right then, as if he were a hypnotist snapping his fingers, his audience seemed fascinated.

"Wow. Really? Good, good, good."

"Yes," Brother Louis continued. "He was very nice, and he said that there are other people he may want to talk with while he is in town."

"Who is that?" Suddenly Venus appeared at the bottom of the ladder. She was wearing what looked like an old high school band major's military-style satin jacket with purple velvet pants. The brother could tell that she was quite proud of herself and was expecting a compliment.

"You look quite nice, Venus," the brother said. "Very cool."

"Thank you," she chirped, then of course, she spun around, which the brother was beginning to think was not so charming but some kind of Tourette's-like nervous tic. When the brother looked over at her father, Bobby was almost pale, rubbing his red-rimmed eyes.

"Did he say who he wanted to talk to?" Bobby got up and started picking up books and magazines from the floor and from the top of the bookshelves. "Man, we have company, E. Why didn't we clean up, god damn it?" He started taking things that he had randomly picked up, including bits and pieces of writing paper, and stuffing them into notebooks. He started to take them into the back room.

The brother, now a little concerned that he may have made some kind of mistake in bringing that subject up, said, "There is nothing to worry about. Nobody ever mentioned anything about you or your family."

"My family . . . That cop better not come around me or my family. I don't need the heat sniffing around here."

"Oh, mellow out, Bobby!" Esther called from behind the cooktop as she stirred the brown noodles into the boiling water. "Mellow . . . yellow," she said more softly as she snapped a dry noodle into her mouth.

"Daddy?" Venus said, and her voice carried an uncharacteristic tone of worry. For the first time to the brother's ears, he heard the tone of the woman Venus was to be. "We're not going to have to talk with the police, are we?" she said in a voice of concern.

"No, dumplin', no fricking way," Bobby said, now looking straight at the brother.

"Where are your notebooks, Daddy—you know, the ones with your drawings? You wouldn't just leave those lying around for someone to find."

"Sweetie, there is no need to worry." Bobby jumped up and walked over to put his arm around her.

"Okay, everything is ready! You two come in here and help serve," Esther said with an anxious voice. Suddenly Esther had a bowl of whole wheat noodles and a big pot of red sauce with moose meatballs, whole wheat French bread just out of the oven, and a green salad.

"Let's eat!" she called out, and everyone dished up in the kitchen, then ate at the big table near the window.

GLEN WOKE UP a bit. Bobby helped his wife. Esther talked with the brother about their life in Cold Storage, about living off the ocean and the land mammals. How even though there weren't any moose around Cold Storage, there were some up near Glacier Bay, and how they bartered with friends up there, trading herring eggs and abalone for moose meat. She talked about the northern lights and said that, although they were nothing like what they had in Fairbanks, there were some nights in late winter where you swore you had taken mescaline when you looked up into the sky.

"It was like . . . whoa! Red, green swirls. Some people even say you can hear the energy in the sky like bells."

The brother nodded and smiled. He actually liked how Esther described her life. She surely loved it. She loved the world of the North unconditionally. Then she said, "You know, Brother, I think that nature is God itself. It is everything we know, and it goes beyond what we know . . . into the mystery."

"Well, yes," he said, but she could sense his hesitancy.

"Right on, witchy woman." Bobby smiled from the bundle he was perched on.

"Oh, Mom," Venus said, "don't tell the story about me in the horse trough!"

"It's a beautiful story, and I'm trying to make a point." She brushed her hair out of her eyes. They were almost done eating and the brother could see she still had the same smudge of tomato sauce on her cheek from before the meal.

"You will forgive me if I'm a little drunk . . . I mean, a little high. Maybe both."

The household laughed and toasted her with their glasses, including Venus, who held her glass and smiled beautifully as she said, "Mom, don't tell the story."

"You've never had children?" Esther didn't wait for an answer. "But this one"—she pointed at Venus, and Venus crawled up into Bobby's lap—"this one was born right here in a horse trough in the bathhouse."

"Really?" the brother asked, genuinely incredulous now and leaning over his empty plate.

"You would know then, ah . . . Louis . . . Thomas, you would know, after having that life grow inside you for nine months—nine *uncomfortable* months!"

"Mom!"

"Not your fault, goddess. But to have this beautiful baby come out of you and ease into the sulfur-smelling water. To see her swimming around attached by the cord to my oxygen supply, swimming like a gray otter or a seal, as happy on this earth as she could be. Then, as Bobby cleared her airway and cut the cord, she turned from gray to bright pink, and there she was . . . a land mammal. I swear she only started crying because she was startled that she wasn't an otter. She was a goddess. We have never been happier. I have never been more certain that everything in this world is connected—water, earth, volcanic pressure, my belly, this baby, this man"—she touched Venus and Bobby—"and all that interconnectedness, that THING, that unbelievably HUGE THING, is what you call God."

There was silence around the table. Below they could hear the wind pushing through the limbs of the ancient trees, and the washing of the icy-cold ocean waves.

"I believe you," Brother Louis finally said, "and more to the point, there are millions of people on this earth who agree with you, and I think they love God as much as you and as much as anyone on earth. I'm going to visit a man who reminds me of how compassionate and loving you all are. He is the Dalai Lama, a Tibetan Buddhist. When I go, I will take him gifts, even though we have never met. He is said to be the reincarnation of the god, if you will, of compassion. He believes much in the way you do. Yet there is something more he believes in."

The people at the table were fairly drunk still, but Venus's eyes sparked like a lit fuse. She was curious. "What is more?"

"See, the Dalai Lama and I . . . I believe—and I will ask him this—in the rightness of compassion . . . that in the universe there is a way to justice . . . or at least a sense of what is just. That there is something more than just the world and all the things in it; there is a loving force that helps guide everything toward the good . . . and the just."

"'The curve of the universe is long and it bends toward justice.' That is what Dr. King said," Glen said clearly.

"Then why doesn't God just get off his butt and help people?" Venus asked. "Why didn't he help those people Glen tried to help? Glen acted when God did not. That's what I want to do. If I ever get out of here. I want to act for the just," Venus said as her parents scowled at her.

"Not now, baby," Bobby Myrtle said.

The brother looked at Venus and then to her parents, just to make sure they didn't need more time, and seeing no indication that they were going to continue, he spoke calmly. "There is a very great writer who died right at the end of the Second World War who saw and imagined things as horrible as Glen saw, and she said something like, 'The proof of God's existence is in his absence from the world.'"

"Now that doesn't make any sense at ALL." Bobby stood up and grabbed the wine jug and waved it like a weapon over the table. "Crazy, man, that sounds like selling snake oil."

"Let me show you what I mean. I'm not saying I will prove it, I'm just saying I will explain what she meant."

The brother looked at Glen and asked if they could get to the top of the ridge on the mountain right before sunrise. He walked around the kitchen counter carrying his plate.

"You mean sunrise tomorrow?"

"Sure. Why not? We get some flashlights and candles, whatever, and we make a pilgrimage to the top of the ridge in the dark. Can we do it?"

"We can pack supplies on the ponies, and they can help pull us up! I've done it before," Bobby Myrtle said.

"In the daytime, sweetie," Mrs. Myrtle said.

"You seem like you want to get out of town while this FBI agent is around," the brother said.

"Do we wear clothes?" Esther asked.

"Yes, I think we should."

Venus was hopping on the floor. "Can we bring bells? The ponies wear bells so we can always keep track of them. I'll check with Ellie about borrowing the ponies and the pack saddles."

"I think bells would be lovely," the brother said.

So that's what they did.

At about one in the morning they were at Ellie and Slip's old place unloading gear and rounding up the ponies. George Hanson had brought the people down in his sturdy launch. He had made the trip many times before and had a good strong lamp on the bow. He was rather amused by this kind of outing, remembering himself and his wife having done similar things in the Cascade mountains in Washington. Hiking up to high lakes to skinny-dip and witness the sunrise.

George brought some supplies for himself, so he could stay in the cabin and keep the fire going. He had the key to the MPB, the mouse-proof box, where Ellie and Slip kept the saddles and bags of grain. He helped Venus get both ponies saddled up with pack boxes and bells around their necks. Venus would either ride on top of the pack saddle or lead the mare, and the gelding would naturally follow along. The mare would drag two long lines, and up the steepest part of the hill, the four adults would hold on to the lines and let the pony keep pace and help them up a bit. They each had flashlights, and Venus and Esther festooned the tops of the pack saddles with lanterns, which could be hooked onto the boxes with small chains. Venus also wore a kind of silver tiara made out of an old round logger's hardhat, which had candles in little glass jars wired onto it. Each person wore a different-toned bell attached to their own belt or blouse, so when they took off in the darkness, they seemed like a lit carousel or perhaps a gamelan clattering up the hillside making sacred music. If there were bears in the dark woods, they would surely move out of their way.

Glen and Brother Louis clung to the same rope behind the mare as they eased steadily up the hill. "Why are we doing this, again?" Glen asked.

"I want to illustrate what Simone Weil meant when she said that the greatest proof of God's existence was his absence from the world."

"Okay," he said, "that's what I thought."

For about forty minutes, the little procession wound its way up the switchbacks that crisscrossed the face of the mountain. The lights from their lanterns cast thin bubbles, which barely touched the ground. The brother stumbled several times, but the small stones and root wads cushioned his fall. He heard Bobby and Esther scrambling behind the gelding and laughing, humming to themselves at times. By the time they came to a ledge where the trees were beginning to thin out toward the alpine, Venus pulled back on the reins of the mare, and the tintinnabulation of the bell, which clouded the darkness like a flock of songbirds, slowed and quieted. In the darkness, the ponies sneezed and stomped their feet on the ground, which was harder now as they got higher and farther from the river. The brother could smell the sweat from the horses, and his own shirt was damp. He groped his way around the mare and bumped into Venus, standing on the other side of her. Her candles had guttered out.

She said, "We should rest a bit. The footing will be better from here right up to where we can make a camp near the little pothole lake. We'll leave the ponies there and make a small camp, then we can climb up the last little bit to the top of the highest part of the ridge."

Again, here in the darkness of the tree, Venus sounded like every person she would ever be: child, woman, mother, or grandmother perhaps. She seemed like all women to the brother.

"We are making good time." Esther's voice came up from behind. Her lantern was turned on. The brother saw his little group inside this bubble of light. A slight wind began to hiss through the trees below them.

"I'm going to put my jacket on. Here, drink some of my

water." They passed Esther's canteen around. "This is great, man. I'm glad I came on this adventure," she said, as she took her drink at the end.

"Hell, yes!" Bobby Myrtle said, as he drank something from another flask. "What are we gonna do now?"

"It will take another half hour to get up to the pothole lake, then we'll unload and get ready to scramble up to the top a half hour before sunrise," Venus said.

"That's good, we should be up on top when the sun breaks over the mountains."

There were a few stars showing up through the canopy of the trees, but there were still some clouds drifting like black icebergs in the sky.

"Can you give us a clue, Brother? Are we going to see God, man?" Bobby chuckled.

Their faces were glaring white in the direct light from the little lantern. The brother looked at them with love and truly felt love in his heart for each of them in their own way.

"Okay," he said, "let's imagine something. Bobby asked if we were going to see God. Let's imagine we already are with God. We have been walking through God all this time."

"Woo-hoo, amen!" Bobby whooped.

"Amen, indeed." The brother laughed. "Remember God's first words in Genesis?"

"Let there be light," Glen mumbled.

"Correct. Before existence, before light, there was God. Let's pretend for right now that this darkness IS God. It . . . it's okay to think of God as an 'it' at this point. There is nothing else but God, and God is in darkness."

"What about our candles?" Venus asked.

"Well," the brother said, "technically there is no 'us' yet. So we don't exist, see? We don't need candles . . . and, no, Venus, I know you are going to ask, there are no ponies yet, no mountain now. On the rest of this hike, we will just listen to the bells. I suggest in order to get the most out of this part of the adventure, just feel your own breath go in and out. We

will feel our feet pull our bodies up the hill, but we will try
not to have a human thought." He reached his hand out and
put it on top of Glen's shoulder.

"This is important for you, Glen. Okay? No memories.
No images from the past allowed in your head. If they crowd
your head, just count your breaths or say 'in . . . out' as you
take each breath. No thoughts, okay? We don't exist now.
Only God exists. Only the darkness. Everybody okay with
this?"

"Can I ask God questions?" Glen muttered.

"No, buddy, not now. We don't exist in this adventure.
We are nothing. If we are anything, we are shadows—dark
shadows blended seamlessly into the darkness."

"Far out," Bobby said.

"Everybody have gloves," Esther asked, "for holding on
to the ropes?"

Everyone did have gloves, except for the brother. At first
he thought he wouldn't ask for them, but to his surprise he
had already worn a blister into both palms, so he accepted
Esther's extra pair.

Everyone turned off their lights except Venus, who held
on to her plastic battery-powered torch. She began leading
the mare by holding on to the halter rope, having taken off the
bridle and reins.

Once again, the thin sound of the bells floated up into the
night forest like prayers. Venus called out obstacles in their
way, giving each pilgrim fair warning. The saddle leather
squeaked and everyone stumbled along.

The ponies made slow progress, and eventually the
brother felt underfoot that they were no longer walking on
a beat-out trail. The footing was hard and even for the most
part, but very steep in several places. The ponies started
lunging up the hill so that their bells clanged faster than
their usual tempo, and the gear for their temporary camp
clattered around inside the boxes. The gelding stopped
and ate periodically. He would take alternative routes for

a few yards, but he never drifted far from the mare. Bobby and Esther let go of their ropes and followed the bells, but Glen and the brother held tight. The brother focused on his breath, trying his best to banish all thoughts, memories, or stories he had told himself about what he should expect to come next. Though he did wake up when he thought he heard Glen weeping. He stopped for a moment and Glen bumped into him.

"Are you all right?"

"Yeah . . ."

"Good," the brother said, then turned to go on.

"But there is no me, and there is no you."

"Yes," was the only reply Glen received.

Soon the sky began to lighten enough that they could make out a ridgeline above them. The black silhouette of the mountain appeared as a hump with the sky becoming almost navy blue above it; the sky a different kind of dark, just enough to be set off against the shadow in the hill. There was one more steep pitch where the ponies rattled and rang, and the brother held tight to the rope tied to the mare. Her breath was a bellows and the damp air smelled of lathered sweat around her rigging. They lunged for ten yards and then it was flat. The pilgrims then saw a dusting of stars salted out at their feet, where the still water reflected the faint light of the coming day.

They were at the pothole lake where Glen and Venus unpacked the ponies and stripped off their saddles and blankets. Glen dug into one of the pack boxes and took out another canteen and five peanut-butter-and-jelly sandwiches Bobby and Esther had made down below. The brother was tired and leaned against the wooden pack boxes, eating the rather crushed sandwich and sipping cool water. Venus let the naked ponies run loose with only their halters and bells on. She had put a pair of sturdy hobbles on the mare to keep her from running far. The first thing the ponies did was roll in the heather and bunchgrass near the lake.

They luxuriated in scratching the sweaty hide on their backs where the saddles had been. The brother could barely make out their forms, but he could see them as vague marionette shapes against the ground as the sky lightened. All of them changed out of their sweat-soaked shirts and put on an extra layer of warm clothes for the push to the top of the ridge.

No one said a word, but soon the four of them were all standing around the brother, waiting for something to happen. Bobby, Glen, and Venus wore small backpacks. They said nothing. Venus had on her hard hat crown with the candles lit. The brother looked at her, smiled, nodded, and stood, then they began the last push.

The brother had fallen in love with M, and he had been wracked with guilt. He had seen a psychoanalyst and even used his doctor's office on two occasions to have trysts with M. He wrote sparingly about M in his journals. He acknowledged he could not reconcile his feelings for her with his duties as a Cistercian monk. Yet his love was not based in lust and could not possibly be sinful, because she herself was so good. This, of course, is what all foolish lovers from the time of Shakespeare's plays on through history have insisted. The brother knew he was a fool and would be judged a fool, or worse, as time went on.

But here, he began to see Venus not as an American teenager, but as a sprite from *A Midsummer Night's Dream*. On that night he followed Venus and the lights on her helmet up the hill, where at the summit he would try to reveal the mystery of both God's omniscience and His absence, as Louis's heart beat like a steam engine in his chest.

# 9

# "LOVE LOOKS NOT WITH THE EYES"

Down the hill, George Hanson was reading by the wood-stove in Ellie and Slip's old cabin. He liked being ashore and enjoyed hearing the wind blow through the trees while his sturdy launch lay firmly tied to a dock and his big boat was secure in the harbor. He loved his new life living on the water, but he still slept better onshore: no concerns for dragging anchors or miscalculated tidal changes. The solid earth, in fact, made him drowsy.

But tonight, as the others were listening to the bells in the darkness, George was reading through a packet of material a friend of his on the Seattle police force had put together and sent him as a favor. His friend was named Skinny, and he had been a very young officer back when George had been a detective. Skinny had been around during the rough days when George and Emily's son had died and Emily had taken her own life. Skinny came up to Alaska several times, and even remembered the hunt for Ellie and Slip that took George up the coast. George was sixty-two years old and Skinny was only in his midfifties, but Skinny had worked his way up to the head of the detectives' section, where he supervised investigations and had good contacts all across the country.

As soon as George had heard about this Brother Louis coming to Cold Storage, George had written to Skinny asking for background information. Skinny had told him

about the Louisville FBI office's intense interest in Louis as a
Communist sympathizer and the head agent's desire to "wrap
him up" with a good case before he left the country to meet
with what he was certain were Chinese agents. Skinny had
also mentioned that Agent Boston Corbett would be sent to
Alaska to "brace" Merton and hopefully delay the Asia trip
before the bigger case could be made. This first package of
information showed up on Annabelle's plane with the rest
of the weekly mail delivery weeks before Merton showed up.

Skinny's second package was sent by a courier to the
Juneau Police Department on a military plane, and then
hand-carried to the Juneau seaplane base and handed
directly to Annabelle. It arrived in three days from Seattle
and was marked "urgent."

The urgency had nothing to do with what Skinny had
found out about Merton, who by all accounts was what he
said he was: a Catholic brother, writer/poet, and an advocate
for peace in Vietnam. The brother was worth keeping an eye
on, but this did not trouble Skinny much. The urgency was
further news from Louisville about Boston Corbett.

The letter was clear and written mostly in bullet points.
Skinny had never been much on narrative, especially in
this message, which essentially said: Boston Corbett was no
longer an FBI agent but had been given an early and unexpected retirement offer in mid-April after the assassination
of Martin Luther King Jr. Skinny had added a parenthet-
ical describing MLK as a "preacher, colored activist for civil
rights, and longtime target of the Louisville office." Boston
Corbett had been the field agent in charge of the bureau's
MLK "background" project. They had wiretapped the reverend's phones, both at home and while he was on the road.
They had recordings of the reverend talking with his girlfriends, talking with scores of political leaders, and talking
with Lyndon Johnson. Skinny wrote that apparently this was
all okayed by warrant.

Corbett had many informants sending him information,

including a photographer who was close to King. Corbett was also known for having close contacts among "the KKK and white racist advocates all across the South and, indeed, in every town where the reverend had ever worked for more than a week." The problem was this: with everything he knew about King, why hadn't Corbett gotten wind of the assassination attempt ahead of time? Skinny had written in his crooked handwriting, *Even in J. Edgar's FBI, such an obvious screwup would be bound to give the director a black eye . . . so Corbett had to go.* Apparently they started burying all the King memos and reports—the famous federal 302s and handwritten notes—in the darkest, most faraway filing cabinets in Washington, DC.

The packet contained copies of some of Corbett's 302s, which Skinny was somehow able to get from Louisville, all because Corbett was still flashing his federal ID and badge around, even after he was no longer with the good guys. This was a serious crime, and surely would be "only undertaken for some . . . nefarious or illegal action." This was what excited Skinny about Corbett coming to Alaska.

What most worried George Hanson were the notes included in his package where Corbett had listed some of his informants with numbers instead of names. The informants were apparently broken down into groups. One group was labeled *Entourage,* one was marked *Hollywood,* another *Chippies* (for one-night stands?), and the last was marked *Girlfriends* (for repeat meetings?). There were attempts to suggest connections to James Earl Ray, but most of them were crossed out. The shooter was usually noted as JER.

George cleaned his glasses and sat up in the chair. It seemed to him that the FBI was sending women to the reverend. But what stopped George Hanson short that night was a very small notation on the margin of one page. *The Lincoln Conspirators.* Here he had underlined their FBI signifiers and the names Spangler and Atzerodt. Then the notation:

*Material support for JER?* This note seemed to be written later and was not crossed out.

"The Lincoln Conspirators?" George said softly to himself. Then Dot woke, barked three times, stretched, growled softly, and settled back into her place by the fire.

"I don't like it either, sweetie," he said, and rubbed the warm right ear of his faithful dog.

Dot was allowed in the cabin and was sleeping next to the stove. Dot was not as comfortable onshore as George was. George had often observed that he had never known a dog as smart and attentive as Dot, which was an advantage on a boat where every little sound—a rattle of the anchor chain or bump in the deck rigging—could mean some possible disaster. Dot alerted George only when those sounds rose to a level of concern, and she never seemed wrong in her judgment onboard. But on land, every creak of a bending tree or rustle in the brush nearby could wake them both from sleep. George often thought it was the smell of the bears in the creek that put her senses on edge, but he could not be sure.

GEORGE HANSON, ASLEEP in the chair by the stove, was awakened by Dot's barking at the door. He stumbled up and opened the door to a clear morning. The sun was well up over the mountains, and far up the hill behind the cabin both George and Dot heard the tinkling of bells.

George made coffee and started cooking bacon on top of the woodstove. He didn't want Dot to go up the hill to either spook the ponies or become entangled in the feet of the hikers. Dot loved people and animals too much, or perhaps it was her urge to herd everything that made her a nuisance in close quarters, and a pony even moderately packed on a narrow trail coming down a steep hill was definitely close quarters. George told Dot to come back inside and stay by the open door, where the one-hundred-pound dog sat shivering, listening to the bells grow closer. A brown bear lumbered into view and made its way toward the heavy post barn where the milk cow and steer were locked in their stalls. Dot began to whimper, wanting nothing more than to go out and investigate. George brought her a bowl of old salmon meat with some of the bacon grease dripped over it.

"Stay, sweetie. Good, Dot," George said, patting her head, and then hooked a long lead to her collar and motioned for her to come with him. They walked into the field, and when Dot first woofed at the brown bear, it stood up in the tall grass.

"Heel now," George said, and Dot cowered by his side. The bear's poor eyesight caused him to squint and tip back and forth on his hind legs. George moved over a few compass points to be exactly upwind of the bear, when almost instantly the bear dropped and lunged, running toward the creek, flattening swaths of grass and even some alder saplings that kept growing up on the edges of the shoreline.

Up on the hillside the bells kept coming closer until George was sure he could hear them directly through the clear summer air of this northerly weather. The bells sparkled now, and finally he heard Venus's voice rise up above.

"Hey, Dot! Hey, Dot. Dot. Dot!" Her voice as clear as a ringing bell.

Dot shivered harder now, whining to be released. Mercifully, George bent down and unclipped the lead from the collar. The big dog galloped, long-legged and stretched out, not unlike the way the bear had run, but the dog ran straight toward the bells and the girl's voice. In a few moments, it seemed as if the bells and the steady clomp of the ponies' steps landed at sea level and the procession entered into the field. Dot was running out ahead, then darting back to push up against Venus's legs, then back out, turning loops and rolling in the grass. Glen and the brother took off their hats and waved them high over their heads at George as the old police detective waved back and headed toward them to take the pony's lead.

Everyone was tired yet still exhilarated from the trip up

and down. None of them had slept. George took Venus's pony and led her to the front of the cabin's porch and started to unpack. Bobby and Esther danced a bit in the field, then came to help.

"Thank you, George," Esther said, a broad smile on her face.

"Good trip?" George asked.

"George, it was fantastic. Really."

Bobby helped pile gear up onto the porch. He, too, was smiling and doing a little jig. "Is that coffee?" he asked. "Can I grab some? May I get some for you, George?" Bobby said, his eyes sparkling as if he were high, but he seemed too happy and energized for George to think he was stoned.

"Of course, Bobby. There is bacon cooking too."

"Dead pig . . . far out . . ."

"I'll get the eggs and toast going," Esther said, grabbing a bucket and heading inside to draw some water and wash up.

Venus was almost asleep, leaning against the pack box. George scratched her on the head like a grandfather might pat a baby, causing her to smile.

"You look happy," George said.

"I am, Mr. Hanson. I learned something and saw something . . . It was more than just pretty. I can't really describe it." She looked around the place as if just waking up. "I don't know why it makes me sleepy."

Venus closed her eyes, but her face was full of afternoon sunlight, and the teeth in her smile seemed white and straight. She looked perfect.

The other two men were standing apart from the rest of the group. The brother had caught the gelding and undone his halter rope. The slightly bigger pony was feeding on the grass and shaking his head.

The brother was talking softly to Glen as George approached them, and all George heard was, "There is no inherent sin in earthly beauty. The church has never said otherwise."

The brother stopped speaking when he heard George walk up. "How was your night, Mr. Hanson?" he asked the old cop.

"I got a little crick in my neck, falling asleep in the chair reading, and the dog was rustling around dreaming. She was hunting bears, I guess."

"Where do you want this gear?" The brother nodded toward the gelding. "It's mostly sleeping bags and leftover horse feed, bells, and hobbles, I think."

"We'll take those out to the barn and put the rigging in the mouse-proof box."

Glen smiled at the ground, deep in thought perhaps. "I'll go get the other pony," Glen said.

"No, we'll take care of it. Why don't you help Esther with breakfast? Brother Merton and I will water the ponies and let them feed a bit."

There was a small clattering inside, where the family was gathered working on their late breakfast. George and the brother walked toward the mare, who was grazing on the north side of the cabin, dragging her halter rope. George took the mare and the brother led the gelding. The men started leading the ponies toward the barn. Dot was curled on the porch next to Venus, who appeared to be sound asleep now. Dot's head rested on the girl's stomach and Venus's hands rested over the big dog's neck. It appeared that she had fallen asleep while petting Dot.

"You must have been reading a good book," the brother commented.

"You mean because I fell asleep reading it in my chair? No. I wish I had been. I was reading police reports."

The men tied the ponies to the barn poles, unpacked the gelding, and secured the boxes and saddles. They brushed the ponies' backs and led them to the water trough beneath the overhang. The ponies took long drinks of the cold water, which had come from a lengthy black hose that ran from the river. It was then that George and the

brother exchanged information about what they each knew
or suspected about the "Lincoln Conspirators."

It seemed strange and sad to George, when he thought
back on it later, that their conversation was taking place on
this idyllic day, when the group was so happy and at peace
and the ponies were warm from their efforts, noisily drinking
fresh water with their lovely movie-star eyes closed in gratitude. In contrast, the information they were discussing was
dark and violent, bringing death to this little Alaskan town.
There was an echo of history, George thought, as clear now
as it ever was, even in the fjords of Alaska—an echo that was
still capable of triggering avalanches.

They talked about the Lincoln Conspirators who had gone
out fishing with Slippery. They talked about the mummy, and
the FBI agent who seemed to be asking the brother to keep
silent about Corbett's interest in the subject or risk having
the FBI "wrap him up" as a Communist.

"So, Mr. Hanson, what do you recommend?" the brother
asked, leaning over the withers of the gelding.

"No crime has been committed so far, other than a man
impersonating an FBI agent . . . unless Skinny got the date of
his retirement wrong, which I don't suspect he did."

"What do you think this Boston Corbett fellow is up to
then?"

"I don't know." George started brushing the mare. "Most
crimes are about the big two motives: love or money. Maybe
Mr. Corbett is upset about his lost job. That could tie into
both: the love of his lost cause . . . working for the bureau . . .
or maybe just the loss of his salary."

"I thought you were going to say the noble lost cause of
the Confederacy." The brother was brushing the gelding's
sweat-soaked back.

"Maybe I was," George said as he unbuckled the halter,
then slapped the mare's haunches for her to trot out to the
pasture. She rolled, kicked the silver crescents of her shod
feet up into the air, grunting . . . happy for now.

"It's possible he came to find his informants. Maybe he wants his informants to keep their heads down and avoid attracting attention. Maybe he wants to silence them so that he won't get into any more trouble. I don't know, but I don't like it," he said finally, as the brother let his pony follow the mare out into the lonely field.

THEY WALKED BACK toward the group in silence. When they entered the cabin, almost everyone was sound asleep, two in chairs and Bobby on the rug with Dot. Only Esther was awake doing some dishes and keeping their breakfast warm on the cool end of the woodstove.

"It looks like we might as well spend the night here again," George said, "unless you have some urgent need to get back to town?" George asked both Esther and the brother.

"That's fine," the brother said softly.

"I've always loved this place. Be glad to stay here a bit longer," Esther said, handing them their plates and pointing to the coffee pot on the stove.

SO, THEY STAYED. Esther pieced together a meal from some salmon steaks that George had in the little cooler in his launch. She made biscuits and some potatoes from Ellie's garden, which was a bit overgrown and badly in need of weeding. The rest of the campers woke up soon enough. It was decided that the family would sleep in the cabin and Glen and the brother would stay in the barn loft.

"Oh, darn it." Venus pouted a bit. "I love sleeping up there. I love hearing the ponies eating their grain."

"Well, sweetie," Esther said, "you are just going to have to make do with sleeping in a nice warm bed."

"Okay," she said, letting out an entire deep breath.

George decided to rig his cot in the launch and cover it over with a big piece of canvas that he kept just for the occasion of sleeping out. The bears, when they were thick in the river, would sometimes walk out onto the dock and mess with the smaller boats tied there. They would chew on gas cans or tear into a cooler looking for a bright fresh salmon, though it was not much of a problem when they were so well fed on the spawning stream fish. George had slept in his launch many times, and Dot was very alert and would usually frighten the bears off if they took a single step onto the dock. George would keep the long lead on her, not wanting her to go off chasing a bear in the darkness.

George had called town on the radio and told Slip their plan. Slip sounded a bit anxious and asked George to be sure to come back in early. He'd said that both the Coast Guard and the FAA were issuing storm warnings, predicting the weather to turn from the south with a deep low pressure rolling in. The news was causing some consternation with his guests. He'd mentioned that the situation at the bar was "getting wet already," a kind of personal code for a lot of hard drinking going on.

"We could use you here, friend, that's all I'm saying," he said, which was also a hint that trouble was brewing. Slip could not speak freely, so he used code, something that was very common among friends in the fishing fleet because everyone could listen in on both sides of the radio transmission. Fishermen had codes worked out with their most trusted friends in order to share information on fishing without giving away the good fishing areas to the entire fleet. The thing that made George a bit nervous was that when Slip called him "friend," that meant Slip was deadly serious and was worried that something bad was going to happen. Both Slip and Ellie would really like George to come in, for reasons that couldn't be gotten into over the fleet's open line. George made up his mind to wake early and get the group going as soon as possible.

That night the brother did dishes with Glen. George did not talk about the information that he had gleaned about the FBI agent. He only mentioned that Mr. Corbett was still in Cold Storage, and he would probably be staying on the boat with him the next night, so they could go out fishing for a day.

"I heard that if you don't talk with FBI agents . . . you know, if you tell them that you want to consult a lawyer or you just don't want to talk with them, they can charge you with obstruction of justice. Is that true, George? Can they pretty much force you to talk?" Bobby asked as he and Esther started drying their hair by the woodstove while Venus was combing out her hair with Dot snuggled up next to her on the couch.

"No, that's baloney," George said. "What? You hear that in jail somewhere?"

"No, George, I've never been in jail. You know that!" Bobby sat up straight like a parrot on a perch.

"Okay, well, no, or I should say it depends on the circumstances. If they can prove that you knew something important, you know, if you had evidence of a crime and you did or said something to throw them off the scent, if you were telling someone not to talk, or you purposely sent them on a wild-goose chase, then . . . then they might charge you with obstruction. But not if you just invoke your right to counsel or to remain silent. That's not obstruction."

"Okay . . . and the FBI only investigates federal crimes, right?" Bobby was sober now. He was sitting up straight and both the brother and George noticed a tension in his voice.

George smiled broadly and said in the nicest possible way, "Right. Say, for instance, if someone had some marijuana they grew in their cabin and the adults in that cabin smoked it occasionally for their personal use, an FBI agent would not be investigating that unless they were really pissed off at them for some other reason that involved the transportation of illegal activity or evidence of such illegal activity over state lines. Then the FBI might get involved. Is that what you are worried about, Bobby?"

Everyone in Cold Storage knew that Bobby grew four pot plants in the window of his cabin, because they could be seen clearly from the water. Teenagers scanned the windows with binoculars from their skiffs, keeping track of the health and the budding of each crop. Even so, no one had ever disturbed or even asked about his plants.

"No, not at all. You know me, George. I never—"

"Save it, Bobby. This guy did not fly out here from Louisville, Kentucky, because of your four scrawny plants."

"Then . . . wait, do they really look scrawny? Never mind," Bobby said, then grabbed the small backpack he had brought from home. "Then why did he come all the way out here?"

"I don't know for certain. I suppose I will ask him when we go fishing."

"He wants to check out Brother Merton here for being a Commie peace freak," Glen said from over by the sink where he was drying dishes.

"Are you really a Communist?" Venus asked as she looked out from under her hair, which had a pink plastic comb tangled in it.

"No," Brother Merton said with his hands in the soapy water. "If I'm anything, I suppose that I'm not fully and appropriately anti-Communist enough," he said, smiling at the girl.

"But . . . what if . . ." Venus started, and then stopped when the big dog started licking her face. She started laughing, pushing her away. "Dot!" she said.

"No more questions tonight. I'm going to set up my bed in the loft," the brother said as he dried his hands and hung the towel on a hook by the fire.

"Okay then, you should take Dot with you. She will warn you if any big animals come near." Venus leaned forward, combing her hair all the way over her head. The small of her back was peeking out above the sweatpants she was wearing, and the brother found himself looking at the opening of her shirt where he could see her strong shoulder muscles curling down her arms and torso. He quickly turned away.

"Dot will be with me," George said. "We're going to bunk out in the launch."

"Okey dokey," Venus said. "Have a good sleep out there." She cradled Dot's head in her hands and said, "I wish you could sleep with me. Dot. Dot. Dot." Then the big dog licked her face one more time before jumping off the couch and bounding over to George, who was standing by the door.

"Good night to you guys. I will be up and around early because we should get home. I heard that the weather wants to turn later on tomorrow. As much fun as this is, I'm not looking forward to getting stuck out here." Then George pulled his flashlight out and opened the door. The brother was right next to him and followed him out.

They walked the trail to the dock together. "You suppose Bobby is really nervous about Corbett, or is he just a little paranoid?" the brother asked.

"Bobby is just that way. Everyone knows he smokes pot. Some of the old folks call him a hippie, but none of them think he brings in any real amounts of dope. Some people are worried a bit about Glen—his drinking—and they heard too many stories about Vietnam and heroin and those kinds of drugs. But they work hard. The Myrtles work with the kids and they also fish. They're friendly and can always be counted on for help when you need it. Though, I have to say that Venus is the best hand I ever had on my boat. She learns fast and that knowledge stays forever."

They got to the top of the ramp down to the dock and stopped. George stood there for a moment watching Dot, wondering what she was sensing. Dot was sniffing the air as if someone was cooking hamburgers, but all the men could smell was the sour, dead stench of spawned-out salmon riding on top of the cold breeze floating down the fresh-water scent of the river.

"But he was acting a little strangely . . . I don't know . . . nervous, I suppose." George turned off the flashlight and they listened in the dark. Gulls were still above the river and riding the mouth of the stream. Eagles sang their broken whistle calls, and about fifty yards away something big was walking through the brush and up the hill.

"I used to think I understood people," George said softly, "but now I'm too old for that kind of nonsense."

Big fish flopped in the estuary before they made their push up into the stream. Soon they would lay their eggs or seed in the gravel and die. The smell in the air foretold the entire story, as the birds and bears competed to profit what they could from the drama.

"Dot and I will roust you boys out of the barn in the morning. We've got to figure out what's going on with our Southern gentlemen. Sleep well, Brother."

"And you too," the brother said, then he turned on his flashlight and headed for the barn.

Glen came along a bit later with a couple of sleeping bags. The brother could smell the marijuana on his jacket, but Glen was moving well and not a bit clumsily as he found a good pile of hay in one corner of the loft, and laid out a canvas tarp he got from the mouse-proof box along with two soft saddle pads from the ponies' rigging. He set down his bag and pulled half the tarp up over himself using his duffle bag as a pillow. Soon enough the brother could hear Glen snoring. Twice during the night, the brother heard Glen cry out in fear. The brother, who was hyper-alert to sounds coming up from the river, sat upright and shone his flashlight over on the sleeping Glen, who did not appear to have woken himself from whatever dream was disturbing him.

The brother eventually gave up listening to every splash in the river. He gave up listening to the ponies and the cattle shift in their stalls. Each grunt or sneeze was a bear trying to crawl up into the loft. Every sound of chewing was a bear snapping bones. And then finally he was asleep.

Not much later he woke up once more to a frantic call. Glen was crying out.

"Up. Up. Up. Up!" Glen said with rising urgency. "Jesus . . .

Oh, no! Jesus," he said again, and the brother pointed the beam of his light once more at Glen. This time Glen was sitting straight up with his head still stuffed inside the sleeping bag. "Up. Up. Fuck, man. Go up!" he said.

"Glen," the brother said, "you are here in the barn. Everything is okay."

"Oh . . . oh. Everything is not okay, God damn it!" the right angle that was Glen's sleeping bag said.

"Yes, it is. You are here in Alaska. You are here now. It's fine. It's fine."

"Okay . . ." Glen said, and he lay back down.

The brother scanned over the end of the loft. Glen was slumped over on his side and appeared to be sound asleep again. Next to Glen, right where he had put it just before he went to sleep the first time that night, was a slim book of poems: *Riprap* by Gary Snyder.

The brother turned off his light. He was sad and conflicted now. He was also very tired. He was about to close his eyes again, but before he did, he noticed a strange glowing ball in the field toward the cabin. He slid out of the sleeping bag, put on his pants and jacket, and slipped on the tennis shoes from his duffle bag, never once taking his eyes off the ball of light that seemed to be floating above the level of the highest grass. He went to the edge of the loft and climbed down several rungs of the ladder where he had a better view below the roofline. He could see the light was moving back and forth as if it were riding on a large animal. He continued down the rest of the ladder. He didn't have his flashlight, but the illumination of the ball was bright enough. He took a step out into the stubble of grass on the edge of the field.

He could see it now. The ball of light was riding on top of the largest brown bear he had ever seen, larger than he had ever seen represented in a painting or a photograph. *I must be dreaming*, he thought, but he wasn't. Neither was he frightened. He was calm. The big bear swayed as it walked. The brother saw the animal's sex, his penis and his testicles

under the haunches. The penis was long, thin. A curved
willow branch curled up and slapped the bear's big belly
as he walked. Drool came from his mouth. The big animal
smelled like the river, except more like the rotten salmon
flesh from the fish gutted and moldering in the woods.

Then, as if that were not troubling enough, he could hear
the breath of the bear, heaving out with a lascivious grunt with
every step he took.

Venus Myrtle's face glowed with a kind of bluish tint, as if
the entire orb were on fire, but her face, throat, and shoulders were the bluest, hottest part of the flame. Venus wore a
red silk robe as she sat astride the bear, her pelvis riding in all
directions at once just behind the large hump of the bear's
shoulders. She was smiling, opening and closing her eyes.
She appeared blissful. The odd thing about seeing Venus
Myrtle this way was that she had ten arms. One hand held a
pistol and another held a fountain pen. All her other hands
held an object: a sword, a trident, a dog biscuit she balanced
on her index finger, a lotus flower, a shining silver crescent
wrench, a bow and arrow, and a pure white clamshell. Her
lips were as red as berries, while her hair was voluminous,
half hanging down to her shoulders and the other half piled
on the top of her head, ornately arranged with something
like lightning bolts pointing in every direction, as if she were
balancing the weight of existence.

Venus smiled directly at the brother, and he felt warm in
his chest. Now he was uncomfortable . . . perhaps embarrassed, as if he had walked in on her during a private
moment. He didn't want her to see him standing there
staring. She was not a girl anymore but a war goddess.

The bear came right up to him, its breath a banquet of
stink in the brother's face. The brother fell to his knees and
put his hands together in prayer. The goddess threw all the
objects away from her body. She was disarmed. Clearly, she
had been born beautiful and fully grown. She was never a
child. She was meant to do battle with the water buffalo god

Mahisha. Here she was, right here, right now on a grassy isthmus in southeastern Alaska. The brother said the Lord's prayer two times, then began with the constant prayer until he started to numb his mind and his body felt heavy as lead.

The bear groaned, as if exasperated. The stink of rancid fat brought the brother back to reality.

"Stop!" the bear bellowed.

Venus shook her head as if to say "no," yet still smiled sweetly down from her radiance straight into the poor monk's grieving heart.

"Stop," the bear said more softly this time, in a voice as deep and plummy as an earthquake. "She is unafraid," the bear said clearly in unaccented English, which seemed peculiar to the monk.

Both the bear and Venus the warrior goddess gave Brother Merton a short bow, then walked on toward the water. The brother stayed on his knees. If he saw where they went, he could not remember later, but that night he believed the bear carried Venus down to the beach, paused for a moment, and swam directly out to sea, where the goddess's light blended in with the white glow of the whitecaps building up with the freshening southwestern wind.

*Lord Jesus Christ, Son of God, have mercy on me, a sinner.*
*Lord Jesus Christ, Son of God, have mercy on me, a sinner.*

THE METER OF the short and constant prayer continued well into the morning when George Hanson finally brought two cups of hot coffee into the barn and set them on the first step of the ladder to the loft, so that the smell would rise up to the sleeping men.

"Daylight in the swamp," George called up through the loft opening. "Drop your cocks and grab your socks," he said, and instantly regretted saying it, considering that at least one of the men he was speaking to was a man of God. "Oh my gosh," he said softly. "I'm sorry, Brother. Anyway, you've got coffee down here."

"How'd you sleep, Brother?" Glen came down the ladder as Brother Louis was standing there, watching George Hanson walk back toward the cabin. The brother was tired and the coffee helped him open his eyes.

"I had strange dreams," the brother said.

Glen walked over to where the ponies were tied and unhooked their halters, turning them out into the field. Then he paused and urinated in the stall. The mare, then the gelding, walked out a few feet and rolled on the beaten-down grass. The gelding stood up and took a long piss, making a bog of the ground as he groaned, then stomped his front feet.

"Sorry, I have those myself. I probably made some noise last night." Glen buttoned the front of his pants and picked up the coffee cup that Hanson had left for him.

"Don't worry about it. Not a problem," the brother said. "But, Glen, I see you were reading a book by Gary Snyder. Do you like him . . . I mean his poetry?"

"Ah." Glen looked around, scratching his uncombed head. "I don't know, really. Venus's dad gave it to me."

The brother let it drop.

Both men yawned and stood quietly watching the ponies feeding. The brother was haunted by his strange dream. It was as if he were waking up from a drunken night of bad behavior, which he didn't want to face in the new morning of promise. He was about to speak of his mood to Glen when Bobby Myrtle came running down the path from the cabin.

"Is Venus out here with you guys?" he asked, a bit out of breath. Glen was about to say no, when Bobby shot past him and climbed the ladder. "Venus! Venus, sweetie!" He crawled up into the loft and looked at both men's sleeping pads.

"Bobby? Is there something wrong? I haven't seen her since last night," the brother said.

"Me neither . . . She is not out here, man." Glen sat on the edge of the feed box.

"She's not around," Bobby said. "She's not at the cabin.

She's not down on Hanson's boat. I figured she must be out here with the horses, or you guys." Bobby was on the edge of real concern. He sounded more frustrated than angry.

"Glen, man, you can tell me. Did you bring her out here? Is she just hiding from me, thinking I would get angry? I'm not angry now, man. I just want to find her."

"Bobby, no. She went up to bed in the cabin with you guys. I went for a little stroll out to the beach, and I never saw her again. I swear to God, man." Glen put on his wire-rimmed glasses and blinked rapidly several times, then stared at Bobby. "I swear."

"He came to bed soon after I got my bed set up, and I never heard anything all night," the brother said.

Bobby walked away without saying anything else.

High above them black clouds traveled out the inlet, casting shadows down on its gray-green waters. A gust of cold wind blustered through the field, causing the green fingers of the grass to tickle the air. Both ponies bucked as they ran, shaking their outsized heads as if they had been bitten.

"Stop it," the brother said under his breath.

"What's that?" Glen asked.

"Nothing," the brother said as he walked two steps away from the barn, where he saw a bear's paw print, wider than his outstretched hand, filled with the gelding's piss.

# 10
# THE BEAST

The cabin was a whirl of activity. Bobby Myrtle appeared to be taking the place apart, looking for clues to where his daughter might have gone. Esther was cooking breakfast on the woodstove. George sat on the porch bench holding a T-shirt and talking with Dot.

"Jesus Christ," Bobby said. "I guess that's the difference between the two of us, Esther. You are happy letting her disappear off into the woods full of bears, and I tend to worry about such things."

Bobby pulled his drawing pad from his pack. The brother had never seen him drawing in it, but it seemed that he liked to keep it close.

"I don't think you should use the Lord's name in vain when Brother Louis is around, Bobby. Besides, you know her. She is around. You have to trust her."

"I do trust her, but she's a kid." Bobby appeared to be about to burst into tears.

"Come on, settle down. Eat something. I will find her as soon as I get everyone fed."

Bobby slumped over his eggs and bread, sulking. "You never listen to my judgment," he huffed.

The brother made his morning greetings, filled his mug with more coffee, and then went out to the porch.

"Atta girl," George said to the big dog. "You know Venus. She's your buddy, right?" The dog was sniffing at a tie-dye

T-shirt that Venus had worn on her climb up the mountain yesterday. George trapped the fabric under his foot, and Dot sniffed and played tug-of-war with it.

"Atta girl," George said again. "Now, go get her. Find Venus."

The big dog sat up very straight with her ears perked up. Her eyes sparkled as if the most fun game in the world was about to start.

"Go on now, Dot. Find your buddy." And the big dog lunged off the porch and ran a few circles in the grass and around the cabin with her nose to the ground. She stopped, perked up again, and then ran flat out toward the trail up the hill.

"She's not a bloodhound, but she will follow a scent if she has mind to," George told the brother as they watched the dog run away. "This might be a problem if she doesn't come back. She might go all the way up the hill, smelling yesterday's scent. Or she might tangle with a bear. She has a ton of intelligence, but I don't know about her judgment sometimes."

"Are you talking about the dog or the girl?" the brother asked.

George smiled and shook his head. "Both, I suppose. I just hope neither of them gets tangled up with a bear. Dot thinks she can whip 'em, and Venus thinks she can talk reason with them."

"Really?" the brother said, thinking of his vision last night and not really wanting to bring it up. He asked, "Have you seen Venus around bears?"

"Oh, yeah. Venus believes all the stories the old Tlingits tell her. She will walk right up to a brown bear and talk to them. I even saw her try to put a ring of flowers around one's neck. The old bear took off running, of course. V was more disappointed than anything."

They sat on the bench while George smoked a cigarette and drank his coffee. Out in the field the ponies were

swishing their tails, and George could hear the broken whis-
tles of eagles calling above the river. Esther and Bobby still
bickered. She called everyone in for breakfast. George got
his plate and went back out on the porch. The brother could
tell he was listening for Dot.

They ate in silence until they heard a braying kind of
barking coming from up the hill.

"That's her." George stood up, put on his pack, and
grabbed a rifle he had tucked behind the bench. "Wanna
come?" he said in a low voice. "Let's not tell Bobby or Esther."
Then he started walking away. The brother was surprised,
but he just laid his own plate down and took off at a jog to
catch up with George.

The barking did not seem to be moving, it just stayed
steady in one place. Dot was clearly up the hill near where
the river narrowed down between two bluffs. They walked
quickly. Bear scat was everywhere along the trail, more so
than the day before, or at least that's how the brother saw it.
They hiked quickly up the switchbacks of the trail. Once they
reached the first bench, George plunged off the beaten trail
straight toward the barking.

Then George stopped and turned. He levered a shell into
the rifle.

"Listen," he said, breathing hard. "Bears get cranky
around something they've taken down and killed. They
don't want to share. If, and I mean if, there is a bear up
here standing over something it's killed, don't do anything
crazy, like running toward it, to pull her away. Okay? Just
look around for a good solid tree you can climb, get at least
fifteen feet up, and stay there."

The brother was trying to process what George was saying
to him.

"You understand? Dot is awfully excited, and she is not
moving. That's all I'm saying. Okay? Let me know you understand, Brother."

"Yes," the brother said finally. "I understand."

They walked toward the howling-barking dog. They heard
the deep roar of another large animal. Not Dot, but something that was close to Dot.

They trotted close to the river. An ancient hemlock tree
was bent over it. About forty feet up that tree, resting on what
looked like a hammock strung between two large branches,
was a web of commercial fishing net. Caught in that net like
a tiny fly was Venus, waving. Not talking.

At the base of the tree was an immense bear. The brother
sucked in his breath.

*"Lord Jesus Christ, Son of God, have mercy on me, a sinner."*

"What?" George asked.

"Nothing, I'm fine," the brother said.

"I should have thought of this place," George whispered.
"Ellie and Slip told me about a tree they liked to climb up
here and watch bears down in the falls below. They built that
little sling out over the river. They slept there sometimes.
They must have shown Venus."

The brother didn't hear a thing George said. He was fix-
ated on the big old bear. It had slobber hanging from its
mouth, and when it turned, the brother could see a long
tapeworm hanging out of its butt. Dot was barking with a
sharp urgency, running in to lunge and nip at the bear.

Venus was yelling at Dot to go away, saying, "Dot! Go home
now!" To the bear, she was screaming, "Stop it, Grandfather.
Dot will not hurt you or your family!"

"Shit," George said. "This is a bit tricky. Don't want Dot
to come running back to us now. Would probably bring the
bear, who is a little pissed off."

The two men went behind another large tree. George
stripped off his pack. He whispered to the brother, "Take the
leash out of my pack. We've got to get Dot. I have to be ready
to shoot. Okay? We will be fine. I don't really want to shoot
this old bugger, but I don't want to lose the dog. Not in front
of the girl. She's too tender-hearted."

The brother smiled at George, who he knew was a

tender-hearted man. He found the leash and said, "Good," then started walking toward the barking dog and the bear.

"Dot, come here now. Come on, lovely." The bear snapped his jaws, so that it sounded like rifle shots. Slobber flew around his head. "Dot. You did a good job finding Venus. Come on, let's go and leave this grumpy old bear alone."

The bear backed up and lunged toward Dot. The dog yipped. She looked over at the brother. The big bear stepped back with his head low to the ground. The muscles in his legs were bunched and as big as tugboat hawsers, perhaps a thousand pounds of bear ready to spring into the air. The bear hopped like a puppy—butt first, front legs second. Dot kept her head down and slunk away as if she were in trouble, as if the brother was mad at her. George signaled for Venus to keep her mouth zipped. The brother clicked the latch of the leash onto Dot's collar.

"Good girl," both men said, and the brother led Dot to the tree where they had been standing. "Good, good, girl." Then George Hanson shot his .45-70 two feet above the old bear's head, and the bear looked at him as if he were merely being impolite.

"She is not yours," the brother said softly.

The old bear turned and dove off into the brush. Both men could hear it overturning boulders as it ran. Dot gave one thin bark and pulled softly against the leash, indicating she wanted to fight.

"You tell him," George said.

Within moments Venus was out of the tree and running toward them.

"I'm sorry. I came up here early, early this morning to watch the bears. When I wanted to come down, that big old bear just planted himself at the bottom of the tree and wouldn't leave. I spoke with him, and I even yelled at him, but he just acted like he knew me or something."

"You did the right thing, V," George said as he lit a cigarette.

Then Venus bent down and put her arms around Dot. "You . . . I was so worried about you, Dot. I thought that big old boy was going to eat you up."

"She did a good job finding you," the brother said, not wanting to look directly at the girl. He watched her hugging the big dog, who was happy now, curling in close to her and licking her face.

"She's a good girl. Yes, you are. I'm sorry for putting you in danger, sweetheart." Venus stood up and hugged George, who patted her back as they embraced. "I'm sorry for making you worry, Mr. Hanson. Thank you for coming to get me." She looked over to the brother and stared at him. "And you too. Thank you for saving Dot. It was brave of you."

When she pulled him into an embrace, the brother kept his arms down at his sides. Her face was against his cheek, and she whispered into his ear, "I saw you last night, standing out in the field. It was so beautiful, wasn't it?"

The brother stood back, startled. "You saw me?"

"It was when I first walked out. I wanted to get up to this bear tree as the sun was coming up again. Like you showed us on top of the hill. I was out on the bench putting my shoes on, and I looked out and you were standing on the edge of the field. Were you praying?"

"I . . . I think so," he stammered.

"I knew it was you," she said.

"Did anything else unusual happen when you saw me?"

The girl looked at him as if he were playing some kind of game with her. Her face was twisted up into a crooked grin and she appeared to be squinting suspiciously at him.

"Unusual? Other than seeing you standing in the field? You must have had a lantern because it was so dark, you know, God was surrounding everything." She smiled broadly, and she reached over and rubbed his back between his shoulders. "But I could see you. I could make out that you were talking . . . um . . . praying."

They stood looking at each other for a moment. Then

the brother took a step backward, his heart beating more rapidly now.

"When your lantern went off, or whatever the light was, I couldn't see you anymore, so I started walking up the hill."

Brother Louis shut his eyes and started saying his silent prayer.

"Are you all right?" Venus, again, touched his back.

"Yes," he said, "I'm fine. The weather is coming up. I think we should get back soon. Your folks were worried about you."

The silent prayer throbbed in his mind as they walked back down the trail. George kept Dot on the lead, just to make sure she wouldn't go bounding off after another bear. Before heading down the hill, he gave her some pieces of bacon he had kept in his pack as a treat for finding the girl.

*Stupid*, George thought as he shouldered his pack and checked his rifle's safety. *Stupid to be walking in these woods with bacon in my pack.* He imagined the bears down by the river swiveling their heads and taking the first tentative steps in the direction their animal desire was leading them.

THERE WAS A quick celebration upon their arrival back at the cabin. Hugs were given all around and a short lecture from Bobby about keeping them informed. They finished off the breakfast, did the dishes quickly, and left them in the drainer to dry. Gear was piled on the porch and packed into their duffels. The ponies and the cattle would remain out in the field. Someone would soon be back to make sure they were safe and the water was flowing. The wind was starting to push the big trees around on the edge of the river. Near the cabin, the large spruce tree rocked back and forth. Its wad of interconnected roots, which lay near the top of the soil, could be seen lifting up as the wind shoved its limbs around.

It wasn't until they started loading the launch that the rain began falling from the black clouds. George rigged a tarp over the forward three-quarters of the launch. A reinforced stove jack allowed the tarp to sit snug around the small diesel's exhaust pipe. George wore heavy rubber rain gear and a green sou'wester rain hat. The others sat with the tarp over their shoulders, their heads out in the rain. The engine, which was positioned amidship, kept their bodies warm.

The waves came at them from the stern, so the wind didn't buffet them too harshly, and the wooden launch rolled easily in the large following sea. Dot did not enjoy the rolling motion but stayed on the seat next to George, sitting up occasionally so that she could see forward. The attentive dog always at the ready. Dot barked at a female killer whale as she sprouted right next to the launch, almost within arm's reach. Venus slowly put her arm out as if to pet the whale, when a second one blew just behind her. This was a much larger male with a dorsal fin that stood some six feet out of the water. The big male's fin reminded the brother of the huge blade of a windmill cutting through the sea. He looked down into the gray-green world and saw the bulbous head of the black-and-white creature swimming just under the surface in the trough of the wave. The animal's eye turned up slightly. As the whale rolled underneath the launch, it caught sight of the brother looking down.

Then the whales were gone.

Venus closed her eyes and pulled the tarp up as if it were a warm blanket. Her expression was blissful. The brother felt a lightness in his chest. Something in his faithful heart felt battered by the vision of the bear and now the whale. He didn't know how, but somehow his faith that God's love was reciprocal was shaken. Suddenly it occurred to him that he was experiencing another creature's relationship with God, and this relationship could be as expressive and real as his own.

The launch lurched forward through the following seas, and the whales resurfaced far ahead of them. The brother, for the first time since leaving Kentucky, felt a type of melancholy come over him, a kind of weakness in his faith. He had felt steadfast standing at the peak as the sun came up on the

mountaintop, but what if there was an entirely separate consciousness he had hitherto been unaware of? What if there
was another form of desire and fulfillment? Could there be
a scripture in another language that human beings could
not and would never be able to interpret? If the Buddha
had been correct that existence was soaked through with
suffering caused by desire, what if there was an entire other
dimension of desire? Did the bear have a Buddha nature?
Did the whales? Even if the powerful creatures never knew
the truth of Christ's love? What was the brother's wisdom
worth if he was never aware of the other dimensions of
wanting? *Maybe God is telling me something by sending me this
lust,* the brother thought as he was held in the palm of this
wild and indecisive sea. Maybe he was nothing but an animal,
with no sacred nature, but only a storyteller's imagination?

THEY WERE WELL soaked by the time they pulled up
alongside George's boat. Dot leapt out of the launch and
swam to the float where the boat was tied. She couldn't pull
herself up onto the dock, but Venus jumped out before
George had stopped the engine and pulled the shivering
dog out of the sea. George and Glen tied the launch to the
mooring float in the harbor, rigged two spring lines to keep
the boat from banging into the dock, while the mooring
lines kept it secure from floating away. Tied like this, the
wooden launch could ride out the battering winds.

The rain was pelting painfully hard. The Myrtle family
grabbed their duffels and a bucket of food that they had
not used, and after hugs and thank-yous all around, walked
quickly toward the ramp and headed home. Glen asked if
George needed any help and was quickly told to go get dried
off. Glen, who was not wearing rain pants and was soaked
through so that his jeans clung tight to his legs, took his pack
and started walking slowly to Ellie's Bar.

"I'll see you boys around," he called as he waved one
hand over his shoulder. The brother could not shake the

melancholy as he watched the former soldier disappear into the rain.

George and the brother went aboard George's large boat. George had wanted to get up to see what had been bothering Slippery Wilson over the radio, but he was also cold and damp and knew whatever the problem was, it was going to take some time to sort out. George stripped off his heavy rain gear and hung it on hooks under cover on the back deck. He then lit the oil stove and dried off with a towel. George gave the brother another towel, lit a cigarette, then pumped some fresh water into the teapot, placing it on the stove.

"It will warm up soon enough," George said, and offered the brother the best place to sit by the stove.

The two men did not speak. Rigging in the boats in the harbor rattled and whined in the heavy wind. The breakwater kept the harbor waters calm, but several small boats had left flags on their sterns, which popped in the wind. The brother was grateful for the silence and felt as if it indicated a kind of intimacy between the two of them, perhaps even a trust. The brother realized his hands were shaking and he was not certain if it was from his thoughts or more simply from the experience with the bear at the foot of Venus's tree that morning.

"Why didn't you kill that bear this morning? I mean, I'm glad you didn't, but what restrained you?" the brother asked, finally breaking the silence.

"Aw, there are lots of guys who would have. There are some old-timers around here who shoot every bear they see, thinking of them as pests to be squashed. But, I don't know. That old fella this morning wasn't really going to do anything . . . Maybe he would have buggered Dot up a little, but that would have been partly her bad judgment—Dot's and Venus's, I guess."

"Are you saying that most people would have killed that bear?"

"Yeah, I suppose. Ellie and Slip don't like that kind of killing. I guess they are right. Bears were there first and, like I said, that old boy wasn't going to hurt us." George tapped the ash on his cigarette in the glass jar he used as an ashtray. "Then there is the problem of the body. The meat isn't much good for eating this time of year. Smells like rotten fish. The other bears will eat the body, but that brings more bears onto the trail and close to the cabin. Ellie wouldn't like that much either."

"The problem of the body." The brother smiled as he said it.

The storm seemed to build as time wore on. Soon enough the water in the teapot began to rumble, and the two men drank hot tea. The big boat seemed to pull against her lines, so George added three more to secure her to the float. The storm turned the sky dark; the brother did not have any idea what time it was. He was feeling drowsy as the main salon warmed up and his clothes dried by the stove. Both men listened happily to the rain as Dot slept soundly now that she was back on her boat.

Both of them woke at the same time to the sound of voices calling, running down the ramp. "Mr. Hanson! Come quick. Something is wrong." It was the girl's voice.

"Hey, George, you there?" Glen yelled after her as both their footsteps beat a tattoo on the planking of the float.

"Aw, Christ . . . I didn't want to sleep," George said as he slowly stood up. Dot was on her feet and scratching at the pilothouse door.

Glen and the girl ran up the dock. Venus's hair was spiking down her head, wet as if she were just out of the shower. Glen's pants were even more soaked and plastered to his legs. His long hair was likewise matted down his neck in the rain.

"Brother, Mr. Hanson. Ellie's place is locked up. No one will come to the door, but there is yelling inside. We tried to get in, but no one will let us in."

"Where is Ellie?" George asked.

"We don't know," Glen said. "The windows are locked and the lights are out, but it sounds like a bunch of drunks are tearing up the place."

"God damn it," George said, and he took his .45-70 out of its case, fed four shells into it, and picked up a handful of other casings from a damp box in his pack. He handed a club used for killing to Glen and looked down at the boy. "You ever broken up a brawl, Glen?"

"Once," the boy said. "In Saigon."

"All right then, let's go," George said. He put on his slicker, made sure he had his smokes and lighter, then hopped down onto the float.

The brother wasn't sure what to do. Dot was obviously going with George, but the brother felt strange staying on the boat by himself, so he gathered up his gear and followed along.

# 11
## CHAOS

There were a few locals outside the bar when they arrived. Mr. and Mrs. Burton, who had lost their son at sea last spring, had heard the commotion and showed up. Wilber Whitman, who appeared to be fairly sober, was there on his bicycle with the boom box in a plastic bag tied to the front of the handlebars. He was not playing his tape of carousel music, perhaps because he was listening to the sound of the argument between several men that was raging inside. It was clearly the Southern gentlemen, but no one could get a view.

"Anyone seen Slip or Ellie?" George asked the group. "Have you seen them anywhere at all?"

Everyone shook their heads. Wilber Whitman spoke up, "I went up to the cabins and called around. Nobody was there, not even that Communist priest guy. He's disappeared!"

"That is me," the brother spoke up, and everyone swung their eyes to him.

"Not a Communist," he said almost under his breath. "Not a priest either," he added.

"Okay . . . got that settled then," George said as he walked over to the front door and started rapping on the wooden panel. Then he walked over by the children's outdoor bench—the shutters were locked up tight.

"Hey! Open up! I want to speak to the owners. Right now!"

The voices on the other side of the barriers quieted some, but there were indistinguishable words spoken and the sound of shuffling feet.

"Hey! This is George Hanson. I need to talk with Ellie and Slip. I need to know that they are all right!"

"They are fine. We are fine. Go away now, please? All right? Bye-bye now." The voice was obviously Southern-inflected and under the influence of alcohol.

"Gentlemen, this is Brother Louis. We have met before. I'm the monk from Kentucky, remember me? One of you bought some bread and fruitcake from the abbey."

Silence.

"You boys sound like you are having a fine time in there. We just got back off the water and were hoping to have a drink ourselves. You wouldn't mind that, would you?"

More shuffling of feet, possible whispering, someone setting up the furniture.

Then the bolt on the door slid back, and the door opened slightly. A pale face appeared.

"Hey, y'all. Listen, I don't know where our hostess is."

George pushed the door open and walked into the darkened bar.

"Hey, honey." The unsteady man looked at Venus. "We were just talking 'bout you, sweetness."

"You stay outside, Venus," George said forcefully. The brother and Glen stepped in behind George, then Glen re-locked the door.

THE INSIDE OF Ellie's Bar was dark. Flames rumbled in the woodstove and the front of the stove was open just a crack so the fire burned hot as the flames sucked in air. George Hanson had his gun off his shoulder, and was now holding it at his waist. The hammer was cocked.

"Turn the damn lights on," he said.

Someone reached over George's arm and placed the fleshy web connecting their thumb and forefinger between the hammer of the rifle and the firing mechanism. George jerked back. At the same time, he heard a metallic click at his ear—the barrel of a small derringer was stabbing into his scalp.

"Easy now, boys, no need for heroics," George Atzerodt said softly. "Ed, search the soldier boy. Let him know that I have a gun at Mr. Hanson's head with the very delicate mechanism pulled back and ready to fire. I am in no mood for a boxing match."

"Yes, sir," Ed said. All of them heard Ed's footfall on the wooden floor. "Now, son, just give me your weapons. Let's be friends here."

Glen gave up the club and Ed threw it toward the pile of firewood.

"Let's all sit at the table," Ed said.

"God damn it. Now, boys," a third man said. The brother recognized Boston Corbett's voice. "This whole situation is just plain getting crazy out of control."

"Sit," the Southerner who called himself George Atzerodt said.

And they all sat in the dark.

"Well, what the heck are you going to do now?" Boston Corbett asked.

"Spare me, sir, if I doubt the sincerity of your concern," one of the Southern gentlemen said from the dark. This comment was apparently directed toward Mr. Corbett. They all settled around the table where a candle was burning, George Atzerodt sitting directly across from Hanson, whose back was to the window on the boardwalk where the curtains were drawn.

"Tell the others who are outside to go home, and that everything is fine. Tell them that Slip and Ellie are here and they are fine."

"Is that true?" George asked.

"Yes, I swear to God they are fine."

Ed was holding the splitting axe in his right hand. He

bent over, opened up the door to the stove wide, then threw more wood on the fire. The light of the fire swung across the room and showed Boston Corbett tied to a chair. His face cut badly, blood spurting from his nose down onto his shirt.

"Tell them to go home." Atz's voice was calm. The words were slurred slightly. He wobbled in his seat. George could smell alcohol, either spilled on his clothes or sweating through them. There were two empty bourbon bottles on the table: "Indian Chief Whiskey from Memphis, Tennessee."

The brother got up and gently slid his shoes on the floor so that he would not trip. He got to the front door, and without asking permission from the man with the gun, opened it.

"We are fine. Slip and Ellie are just taking the night off. We're going to clean up in here and then get something to eat. Should we see you down at the café?"

There was a general atmosphere of relief out on the boardwalk. The adults walked away, and as Wilber Whitman pushed his bicycle away, he turned on his boom box so everyone in the neighborhood could hear the chugging music of an old carousel floating down the boardwalk. The brother told Venus that they were doing great but that she should go home and get some dinner. He was about to close and lock the door when the girl's shoulder slammed against the edge of the door and pushed him back on his heels. His bad back seared with pain. Before he knew it, Venus was inside. Dot had somehow slipped in and now lay by the stove.

"I want to see Ellie," Venus said.

"No!" shouted Glen. "Get out of here, V. Now!"

Venus saw the bloody man tied up. She saw the guest from Alabama holding what looked like a toy gun, but what was the worst was seeing how serious George Hanson's face was. How he didn't look up at her but kept his eyes steady on the hand that was holding the gun. Could George Hanson possibly be scared of something? The thought had never in her entire life occurred to her. She slowly walked over to the long table and sat down next to George.

"Search her," Atz said.

"Don't fucking touch her," Glen said with a cold voice.

"Don't worry about her," the man tied to the chair said in a calming voice, as if he still had some authority in this situation. He spit blood out onto his L.L. Bean boots. "But I would check Hanson there again, for I'm betting he has an ankle gun."

Ed Spangler told Hanson to stand up and walk toward him.

"Can we put some lights on in here?" George asked. "I don't much like stumbling around with a bunch of drunks with guns."

Silence. A long breath, and George was certain that both men were drunk.

"Honeypie, would you turn the lights on in the back of this room? Mr. Hanson is right." Atz shifted the derringer from one hand to the other. The gesture itself seemed kind of comic to the Alaskans. George noticed that it was a large-caliber four-shot revolver. Inaccurate from any distance, but deadly at close range. It occurred to him that Abraham Lincoln was killed at close range by a large-caliber single-shot derringer.

George nodded, indicating that Venus should follow directions, then he walked toward the gunman. "I don't think these gentlemen intend to shoot anyone," George said as he pulled an empty chair out from the table. He put his left foot on the chair.

"Search away."

Atz bent over the chair, shifting the gun from one hand to the other, and just as he was about to pat down George's lower legs, George swung with an uppercut straight into the Southerner's throat and grabbed at the gun. Atzerodt fell backward but the gun remained in his hand.

"Stop it now!" Ed Spangler said. He had a hard face, but his voice sounded scared. The lights came on and Ed was standing near the bar with his forearm around Venus's neck. The icicle flash of a thin blade pulsed against the girl's throat.

"Let's all calm down now," Ed said. "It would break my heart to slice this girl's throat, but I don't see that would be my fault, would it?"

George straightened up. Atz was on the floor, breathing hard and holding his throat.

"Boys . . . all of you! Just calm down. We can walk this back." Boston Corbett's voice was weak. It was possible that he was going into shock from his injuries. "Gentlemen, we have not crossed the Rubicon here. You still have options. We can clean this all up."

Corbett's rant must've caused the men to forget about George's supposed ankle gun—no one went back to complete the search.

Atz stumbled slowly over to the chair by the stove. "Talk, talk, talk. My Lord, Agent Corbett, you do like to talk. We did your dirty work, the Negra messiah is dead, and all you do is keep talking, even after you've outlived your usefulness." Atzerodt started to bring up his arm.

"No," Corbett said softly.

"Wait!" the brother said, ready with an argument for restraint, but Mr. Atzerodt raised the gun and put a .45-caliber slug into Corbett's skull. The brother, who had been wondering about the dynamic of the two Southerners, sat back in his chair. The coward Mr. Atzerodt was the killer. The more dangerous of the two.

A soppy crater of brain matter fell out onto the floor. The former FBI agent's face now looked as if it were a stretched-out rubber mask. His skull having lost its round integrity, the flesh over the cavity of the exit wound hung horribly loose. He was slumped in the chair, his hands and his legs still bound. Dot ran to the corner of the room and whined, trying to curl herself into a ball.

Ed Spangler looked sad. He was holding Venus in his

arms, cradling her sobbing face in his hands to keep her from looking at the scene before them, but she had seen the violence of men now. She would never be able to forget it. "Well, we've crossed the fucking Rubicon now, boys," was all Ed Spangler said.

Spangler took Venus to the table and pulled out another chair, then sat her down. She was just two feet from the corpse. She turned her head away.

"What do you think you are going to do now?" George asked. "We all witnessed you murder that man. Are you going to kill us all? Then what about everyone else in town? Don't you think they will be a little suspicious if you are the only ones who walk out of the bar?"

Spangler cut the ropes holding Boston Corbett's body. He went over to another table and ripped the heavy gingham-printed paper off the tabletop and tied it around Corbett's face with some of the rope. Then he pulled the body back behind the bar. A smear of blood followed the corpse around the corner, out of sight. Venus stopped wailing, then blew her nose on a napkin. She started to get up and move over toward the men at the table.

Mr. Atzerodt replaced the spent casing in his revolver with a new round. "You stay right there, missy. We're going to be leaving soon." He snapped the cylinder shut, then turned back to the men. "Now is the time, gentlemen. The war began before this happened. The war for our nation started months ago, when the Communists and the col-oreds joined forces to take over our freedom. You might say it started with the first war of Northern Aggression. After the Second World War, the Jews and the Communists rebuilt Japan. They rebuilt Germany. What did they ever do for my country? More than six hundred thousand white people died in the first Civil War and nobody ever shed a tear about them. There was no damned Marshall Plan for the South."

"Now wait . . ." the brother said. Ed Spangler now had

George's .45-70 at a waist-high position. He jacked a round into the chamber and the existing one fell out onto the floor. He bent over and picked it up, embarrassed and unsteady on his feet. "You aren't finding some equivalency between that murder you committed and a soldier's death in battle?"

"Just button your lip, Brother. Agent Corbett there was fighting a war, all right. His boss called your precious Dr. King 'the most dangerous Negra in the world.'" He gestured with the gun as if including the entire world within range. "He spied on King and used us to arrange the solution. He used the patriots to do his boss's dirty work. But then when they fire him, he starts wetting his pants like a little girl. He tracked us down here, wanting us to 'lie low.' He was worried that his former employer or someone else was going to figure out his part in the assassination of this 'Black messiah' and put him behind bars. Well, fiddlesticks, this is no time to lie low. We are ready to get our country back. We are ready to arm every white man the Jews have deceived and deserted, and we will do it, sir. But Mr. Boston Corbett says we can't raise an army. We can't steal back the body of our great hero. He dares to tell us no, after we took the risks and got the business done. He wants us silent now at the perfect time for our uprising. No, sir. It's happening."

"What are you doing here?" Venus cried out.

"Oh, honey, we are raising an army. This is a recruiting trip for us. Of course we heard about the body of the great hero of the South that Ellie has down in her root cellar."

"Disrespectful . . . awful," Ed Spangler blurted out.

"Ed, grab me our recruitment bag, will ya?" George Atzerodt kept his eyes on the girl while the taller man went back to the kitchen and brought back a small suitcase. "I tell you that old gal was not gonna sell. I just want to show you people that we offered to buy her old gentleman fair and square. We made her a fair offer, but I think she just took a hard disliking to our proposition." He slapped the case on the very end of the table near where Venus sat. When he opened it up the teenager gave a gasp.

"Holy moly!" she whispered.

The case was plumb full of twenty-, fifty-, and one-hundred-dollar bills.

"Yes, indeed," Mr. Atzerodt said. "You ever seen so much money in your life?"

"No, sir," Venus said softly and almost reached out to touch the cash, but then she recoiled, as if seeing a rattlesnake squirming through the leaf-like bills.

"Yes, ma'am, we would have paid Mrs. Ellie well."

"You didn't hurt her, did you?" Venus asked.

"No, dear, she is safe. Don't trouble your mind. You see, we thought a small town in Alaska where the great man was being held would be a good place to find soldiers for the New South, and we pay our recruits for travel and training and such."

"That didn't turn out so good. We didn't come away with any soldiers here . . . yet," Spangler said. "Just a couple of old Communists, a worn-out ex-cop, and a peacenik pervert of a Catholic monk."

"Just shut up about us," Glen said. "George asked you a question. How are you thinking about getting out of here?"

"I had some hope for you, boy," Atz said. "You've done some killing, and you know that it was all for some bullshit settlement that the Communist government in China will broker with all these weak-livered Jews in government. They will divide up all the dope and rubber and sell it back to the white world at three times the cost."

"Are you going to talk us to death, Atz?" Glen asked. "Or are you talking because you don't have a clue how you are going to get out of here alive?"

Atz stared at Glen. Then he walked over and picked up one of the bottles of whiskey and drank the little bit that was left.

"All I need from you, boy, is a sturdy box about five and

a half feet long with a top that comes off and rope handles on the side. It has to be big enough to hold two bodies, one on top of the other. We'll be giving Mr. Corbett a burial at sea."

"Two bodies?" Venus looked incredulous.

"Corbett and Mr. John Wilkes Booth down there in the root cellar. We're not leaving him behind in this little old town where he is not appreciated."

"Why would we agree to do anything for you?" the brother asked.

George winced, suspecting that he knew the answer already.

"Because if you don't help us get out of here, I'm going to shoot this beautiful girl dead." Atz spoke through clenched teeth.

"I will kill you myself," Glen said.

"I doubt it, son," Atzerodt said. "I've seen your type. They killed you already in that Jewish war. You a dead man, boy. A coward. I'm more worried about old Mr. Hanson here, and he's half played out." Then he turned to Venus and said, "Honey, we're going on a boat trip. We'll be out maybe four or five days. Why don't you get some food together for the three of us? Okay, now, sweetie?"

Venus looked over at George and he nodded that she should do it. "Whose boat you taking out in weather like this?"

"Bright and early we'll be taking your boat, George."

George let that last statement sink in. He said nothing for a few moments. "You'll never make it. You will either run it up on the rocks, or you will come right back here."

"No, we won't be coming back here. If we see any government boats, or if we see any planes flying overhead, we will kill the girl."

"Of course, if you kill her, you lose all your leverage," George said. "Where do you think you are going, anyway? Still a long way home to Alabama."

Ed spoke calmly in return. "We have friends. Didn't I tell

you that we've been on a recruiting trip? We have friends all over who will help us."

"Lots of cops in Ketchikan. The phones and the radios will still be working. Even if you knew how to navigate my boat, which I doubt, there will be cops waiting for you."

"And again, George. First cop I see, the girl dies, and it won't be quick. Hell, we might have ourselves quite a party on our way to where we're going."

Glen started to stand up. His fists were squeezed tight into a ball. "I will tear your guts out."

"No, son, you won't. Now, Glen and Mr. Spangler will go get the box together. Glen, if you call anyone for help or do anything, and I mean anything sneaky, Mr. Spangler here will shoot you through the head. And if you aren't back with the box in . . . let's see"—he looked at his watch—"two hours, I will shoot one of these two men. Understand?"

"This plan will never work. Shouldn't we think of something else?" the brother asked in a soft voice.

"Hundreds of thousands of white Southerners made the ultimate sacrifice for their country. Imagine the Battle of the Wilderness, Brother. Imagine crouching down in a ditch and being told to run across that open field that was blurry with flying lead. Then imagine getting up and doing just that. Seven thousand boys died in just two hours. But what I think of most, Brother, is that six thousand and ninety-ninth. After all he'd seen, the ground sloppy with blood, and the battle almost certainly lost, he still got up and ran out into that field." Atz was breathing hard as he spoke. Sweat ran down his fat face. His thumb was scratching the hammer of the gun.

Everyone stayed silent for a moment. The lights flickered as there was a surge in the power. The fire had burned down to coals, flickering through the open stove door.

"I would be honored to die for my country like that, sir," Atz said, almost in tears.

"Fine," Glen said. "I would be honored to kill you."

"Go on now, boy. You got just a little time. Get me that box," Atz said.

WHEN GLEN WALKED out of the bar, the wind slammed the door all the way open, almost breaking it off its hinges. Sunlight of late afternoon was milky white behind the clouds. Rain pelted down so hard that each drop that hit a flat surface looked as if it were bouncing back up in the air trying to retrace its steps to the sky. Ed Spangler carried George's rifle in a sling over his shoulder.

"We don't have that much time," Ed yelled over the howl of the wind. "Where we going first?"

"I'll get you a box. Don't worry," Glen yelled back.

The boardwalk was empty. People were staying inside during the storm. The two men walked north to the far end of the boardwalk where the cannery sat. It was a huge barn-like structure built on pilings. No boats were unloading now, but a small crew was working at the cutting tables, knives flashing through the red meat of salmon. Some young people with hairnets and white aprons prepared the fish for packing, cooking, sealing, and boxing up for shipment. The two men walked past the slime line where the cutting was done and toward the back where there was a carpentry shop. Most of the boxes were built on-site. Glen opened the door to the sound of hammers driving three-penny nails into wood as the smaller case boxes were assembled. He walked over toward a Black worker who seemed to be in charge. Ed Spangler crowded right in next to Glen to make sure he heard what was being said.

"You just wait here," Glen said to Spangler. "I'm going to ask about what they have, and I don't want you saying any crazy racist shit to this guy."

Bernard Walton was the shop foreman for the carpenters. They built shipping crates and kept the huge timber building fit during the year. He had worked in town for two years, while buying up big logs before the pulp mill got them.

He had ten Sitka spruce logs and four red cedar logs for art-
work decked in the back of the building. He was just working
on a deal for two old Brazilian logs and a big stick of ebony
down along the Amazon. He had no clue how he was going
to transport them north, but that was a problem for another
day. Bernard was to become the town's only permanent Afro-
American. He had already done his army time in Germany
and that had caused him and Glen to become friends.

Spangler had the rifle down, his right hand around the
trigger ring, which didn't seem to bother anyone in the box
shop. He lifted the barrel and pushed the muzzle against
Glen's gut. "Just don't forget. Something goes wrong here and
there will be someone missing at the bar when we get back."

"Jesus," Glen said. "I don't have a memory problem."

Ed sat on a bench near the doorway to the cannery. Glen
spoke to the carpentry foreman. They walked around the
shop and found some shipping cases that were the perfect
width. Glen gestured and Ed could tell they were discussing
the possibility of making one about six feet long. Bernie
Walton motioned to his watch, and Glen took a roll of money
out of his pocket. Ed noticed with interest that it was a fat
roll of bills, uncomfortable in the pocket and too big for
drinking money in this dump of a town.

Glen peeled off five bills and handed them to Bernie,
signaling to his own watchless wrist, clearly pressing the car-
penter about time. Finally, both men nodded, shook hands,
and walked away.

"Thanks, man," Glen said over the din of machines.

"It's cool. Thanks for the work."

It was clear that Bernie was doing this off the company
books and Glen's money was going into the wood business.

Glen came back and sat next to Ed on the bench. Ed did
not look at him but said, "Where'd you get that money roll,
soldier?"

Glen didn't answer for a moment. Then said, "A, it's none
of your fucking business, and B"—he started to take a long

breath to possibly offer an explanation—"B, it's still none of your fucking business."

"Okay, take it easy. When do we pick up the box?"

"An hour and a half, maybe sooner. The guy said he will get right on it. He's got the wood and the jigs all set up. He will just cut some long pieces, double them up for strength, and have his boys bang them together."

"What'd you tell him it was for?"

"I told him I had to ship some fishing gear—heavy line and weights—down to a buddy in Sitka, and George had agreed to sling it into his hold as long as it was boxed up solid, so he could move it fast and easy. I said George was leaving and I wouldn't get a chance to get this to my buddy if I didn't get it loaded onto the boat by this afternoon, that George wasn't going to charge me as long as it was boxed up and delivered to him on time."

"Good story. You must be a real bullshitter."

"So, what do we do now?" Glen asked without much interest and without acknowledging the bullshitter comment.

"Let's get out of here and come back in forty-five. I can't stand being around all these coloreds," Spangler whined.

"What the fuck are you talking about? There is only one Black man on shift right now. Two in the entire town."

"Two too many." Ed picked up George's rifle and made his way out, then turned and waited for Glen. He motioned with the rifle barrel for Glen to follow him. They walked down the boardwalk and back to the bar.

When the two men entered the bar, Bobby and Esther were sitting in the middle of the room. Bobby looked to have a broken nose and Esther was tied to a chair. Blood squirted from Bobby's nose like a split brake line. Esther did not struggle against her bindings but stared up at George Atzerodt as if she could shoot lightning from her eyes and strike him down. Mr. Atzerodt was still holding on to his small gun and was now also holding a bloody bar rag to his right eye.

"My God, what kind of fresh hell is this?" Ed Spangler

asked. He checked that the safety on the rifle was off, then lifted it to his shoulder and moved to the corner of the bar by the back door, making sure he could swing his sights down on anyone in the room.

"We got to start killing people, Ed, because there are just too many dumb Alaskans in one room," Atz said. "This little pistol of mine doesn't seem to frighten them enough."

"Go down to the cellar and get our hosts," Ed said. "I will hold them here."

Mr. Atzerodt dabbed at his eye with the towel. "Come on now, honey"—he waved at Venus with his little gun—"you hold the flashlight and take me down there."

Bobby Myrtle leaned back in his chair and groaned, letting the blood bubble out of his nose.

"Don't you hurt her, or I swear to God . . ." Esther spit her words out.

"Let's just all sit here and relax," Atz said quietly. "We'll be out of your hair in a minute."

Venus raised her hand. "May I go grab some things from my house before we get on the boat?"

"Jesus! You have twenty minutes. In twenty-one minutes, I start shooting people," he said, and looked at Spangler.

"Give me thirty minutes."

Brother Louis laughed out loud.

"No. Jesus H. Christ, girl," Atz said, then waved at her. "You, Brother. You come with me."

"Well, I'm not going anywhere if you don't let me go get my stuff."

Atz's eyes burned into Venus. "Oh my God!" he yelled.

"I'm serious," Venus said, and she crossed her arms and stood up straight.

"Listen," Mr. Atzerodt said, clearly trying to keep his temper while holding a firearm, "you go and come straight back. Understand? If anyone comes to this door, I'm going to kill someone. So don't talk with anyone . . . and don't even think of bringing back any weapons."

"We don't keep weapons in our house," Mrs. Myrtle said haughtily, as if drawing a fine moral point.

"As well as your husband puts up a fight, madam, I think it would be to his advantage to carry a sidearm. Now go, girl. Thirty minutes or I'll kill your father." It was about a quarter past noon according to the clock on the wall above the bar.

Down in the makeshift root cellar, the brother untied Slip and Ellie. Following instructions, Slip carried the Old General up the dark stairs to the bar.

"This is a hell of a lotta fuss for this old dried-out turd," Slip said as he carried the desiccated man.

"Show some respect." Atz was almost whining by now.

"You show some respect," Slippery said. "I'm not gonna give my life for this old pepperoni stick."

Ellie hissed at him from behind. "Slippery Wilson, you are going to get us shot."

"Oh, hush," Slip said. "We been in worse scrapes than this. I'm just telling this peckerwood that he still has a chance to make this turn out better for himself, 'cause waving that little gun around is going to cause himself to get shot . . . or worse."

"I don't think so," was all the gunman said.

Soon enough they were all sitting around the mummy looking at each other—Slip, Ellie, the two Myrtles, Glen, the brother, George, and the two Southern gentlemen with the guns. They were all waiting for Venus.

"All right," Atz said. "This little girl is not in charge of this situation." Then he cocked his weapon and stood behind Mr. Myrtle. "She has two minutes, and then I'm going to shoot you."

"No, man, you will regret it." Bobby Myrtle shivered as he spoke. "Wait on her. She's a teenager. She's always late."

"Maybe so, but I'm not going to regret it at all. I've got too many hostages as it is."

Esther was not so defiant anymore. "Please, sir, wait, please."

Atz poked the muzzle of the barrel into the back of Bobby's skull. "You want to say a prayer, Padre," he said, looking over at Brother Louis.

The brother started with Psalm 23, slowly and with feeling. "*The Lord is my shepherd; I shall not want. He makes me lie down in green pastures . . .*" He continued through the valley of death and on through the rest of the psalm. "*Surely goodness and mercy . . . shall follow me all the days of my life.*" Then he slid into the Psalm 24, "*The Earth is the Lord's and the fulness thereof.*"

Glen began smiling. Finally Atzerodt stepped back and said, "God damn it, that's enough."

Bobby Myrtle had his eyes shut tight and was gritting his teeth in a pale grimace. The blood had just stopped running from his nose.

"This won't hurt, son," Atzerodt said. He straightened up and stood back a bit more to avoid blood spatter on his clothes.

The door slammed open and in came Venus. "I got everything," she said. "I brought some cards so we can play crib." Then she looked at her dad and the posture of the gunman. "Hey, what's going on?"

"Nothing, babyface," Esther finally said. "We're just glad to see you. You just took a little longer than we thought." It was one-fifteen.

# 12
## THE TRIP

The storm was reaching its peak in the late afternoon as the coffin-length box with what was believed by some to be the body of the famous actor and the FBI agent swung wildly like a kite down off the dock as George helped load it in the hold. Spangler was in the wheelhouse with Venus. They had loaded their personal gear and the food Ellie and Venus had put together for them back at the bar. Venus hugged her dad for a long time before saying goodbye. When he tried to kiss her, she pulled away. Then she hugged her mom, but almost pulled back in shock as George Hanson stepped forward to hug her. She stood up on her tiptoes. She felt George's right hand firm on her back and she felt the weight of his ankle gun drop into her coat pocket, but she showed no surprise or acknowledgment of it being there.

"Use it only if they try and hurt you." He leaned back.

"Yes, Uncle George, I will. I promise." She smiled sweetly up at the old police officer. Then Glen stepped forward to say goodbye and Atzerodt stopped him short.

"Can I just run up to the restaurant to say goodbye to the owners?" Venus asked.

"No. We are leaving. Now."

Glen pushed forward. "Oh, let the girl go."

"Jesus. No more. She'll be back home before y'all know it." Then he turned to George. "I'll have someone call Ellie's

Bar when we reach port. They will let you know where to pick up your boat and this girl . . . if I don't kill her first."

"Where're you going?" George asked.

"You will find out when the call comes. We are just going out the inlet and then either north or south. Hell, you might just pick up your boat in Panama or the North Pole."

When they had everything secure on the boat, George said, "There will be a hell of a sea out there. Keep the smooth side down. One last time, I will go with you. I know the boat."

"It would be nice to have you. I notice the tanks are full, and both me and Ed know our way around fishing boats and we're not afraid of water. But I can't trust you, Mr. Hanson. You are a natural-born hero, I believe."

"If you go through with this, Mr. Atzerodt, the next time I see you will be the occasion of your last breath on this earth," George said as the wind nearly knocked him off the dock. He had Dot by his side, who was whining to go back inside and out of the storm.

"You hear yourself, George? A natural-born hero. That's why you are not coming," Atz said.

Ellie gave the girl a side-arm hug and patted her on the back, encouraging her to get on the boat.

"You better make sure she makes it back to us," she said to Atz.

"Yes, ma'am," was all he said.

ATZ CLAMBERED DOWN the ladder on the pier where they had slung the coffin in. It was about ten feet down to the boat. Spangler put the throttle forward and the big bow of the *Phalarope* began to pull away. Venus handled unhooking the temporary mooring lines. George unhooked the big dog's leash and just pointed to his boat and said, "Go." The dog leapt the ten feet and landed on the back hatch. Venus ran back and wrapped her arms around Dot. The boat was hard enough for the two men to handle in the cramped harbor, much less for them to try to bring it back to the dock, so they gunned the engine and motored out to the inlet.

"That dog will keep an eye on things," George said.

Annabelle ran down the boardwalk from her office with a slicker over her shoulders. "Where the heck is the *Phalarope* going, George?" She had to yell above the storm. "In this kind of weather? It's supposed to blow sixty knots tonight."

"It's a long story, girlie." George had long called Annabelle "girlie." "But tell me one thing . . ."

BY THE TIME George and Annabelle got into discussing the foolishness of going out into the height of a major storm, the winds had built to about forty knots with gusts up to sixty. George Hanson stopped trying to convince Annabelle to go up in her plane, but agreed to go out with her at first light the next day. There had been a thought raised that the *Phalarope*'s crew would come back into the harbor after getting their butts kicked on the outside waters. This is what anyone with any sense would do. Either that, or they would have to find a secure anchorage, someplace where they could lay out a lot of chain with extra weights added to hold the *Phalarope* secure. If either of these things happened, it would be a much shorter flight or no flight at all to locate them. The most likely scenario was that the Southerners would capsize the *Phalarope* in the massive waves offshore or put it aground during the night while trying to anchor. But at this point there was nothing to be done about that.

After about an hour, the discussion among all of the upset parties—which now included the Myrtles, who were none too happy about Venus being on the boat—had shifted to what could be done with an airplane anyway, and who was going in the plane. The decision was to first find the boat, and second, not to be seen or heard by the two Southerners. Third, and here is where time going by was in their favor, they would try and determine where the boat was going, and try to get there first without tipping them off.

The Myrtles both favored calling the police until the rest described the shooting of Boston Corbett. They showed the Myrtles the brain matter still on the floor, along with a copious amount of the thick syrupy blood that had spread out as a result of the shot through his head. Even though the gun was small, it had a large bore and a heavy load. This kind of derringer, which was similar to the one used by the Southerners' hero in Ford's Theatre back in April of 1865, was specifically designed to kill a man with one shot.

After some emotional discussion, the Myrtles were convinced to stay behind in case the *Phalarope* returned to Cold Storage. They agreed to wait for three days before contacting the police unless they heard more news. If they heard nothing by then, they would do what was necessary.

Both parents mentioned that Venus seemed too eager to go with the Southerners, and that she took a lot of her personal possessions with her thinking that she was certainly in for a long trip. The only thing she didn't take with her was her record player and her album collection.

As to who would fly, George was always going. Annabelle was going to fly the de Havilland Beaver with the big radial engine, but then Ellie insisted she fly it instead because she was older and "expendable," which caused a further row and long discussion. Finally it was decided that Ellie would fly in the captain's chair and Annabelle would fly in the right chair to help navigate and read instruments if necessary—the pilot would have her hands full just keeping the plane upright and flying straight in a storm. When that decision was out of the way, nothing could keep Slip from going. Glen then insisted on going because he was the only one with recent "combat experience" in the group. This started another argument about what they were going to do when they did eventually find the Southerners. It was agreed that Glen should go, and by that time Brother Louis, who suggested that there needed to be a "moderating voice of reason," was allowed the last seat, mostly because everyone was tired of arguing. Six people in the rugged bush plane would make it heavier but certainly not overweight. The added weight would make it float heavy if they had to put it down in rough seas but also less likely to flip over in a heavy gust. With two pilots, there would be four hands to horse the stick around if it came to that.

George suggested they meet back at the bar at three-thirty the next morning. They would review the weather situation, eat breakfast, and pack a lunch. He asked Glen to bring a handgun, which he knew the young man kept. Slippery only owned hunting rifles. George would bring a handgun and his .45-70 lever action. The two women and four men did not shake hands that night, only looked one another in the eyes to confirm their pact to find the girl and recover the boat. They shared their thoughts only with themselves, then walked off to get some sleep.

The brother did not sleep well that night. The storm battered his small cabin and the trees hissed all around him. Several gusts came crashing in off the water and shook the cabin as if the winds wanted to lift him up and tumble the building down the hill. Wind found every crack in the carpentry, whistled under both doors, and shimmered the candle flame that he was trying to read by. He read scripture, looking for guidance on whether he should throw in his lot with this desperate group. Then he tried reading modern poetry but found no guidance there.

Eventually the brother found sleep. He dreamed of the girl riding the bear. The bear did not speak, and the girl looked at him with a penetrating grin that frightened him. She frightened him more when she came close to his face and opened her mouth wide, showing the dark hole rimmed with white teeth and a wet tongue in the center, then somehow generated the rattling high-pitched trilling of the mechanical bell of his travel alarm clock. The brother dressed quickly, then said his prayer silently as he went down to Ellie's kitchen and looked for the pilot of the plane that would take him out of Cold Storage.

In what seemed like moments, he walked into Ellie's. He was wet from the short walk in the hard rain, but, still, he felt sleepy and dream-soaked. Annabelle was the only one sitting, drinking coffee and looking over a nautical chart. She looked up and started talking to the brother as if they had been chatting all night long. The storm seemed worse if anything, but Annabelle said that was only the effect of the sun coming up, which always brought a freshening for the wind, and she was encouraged by the rise in the cloud ceiling.

"Higher the clouds, the higher we can fly. It will be bumpy, but we should be able to see the earth from a long way up."

"That's good?" the brother asked while he finished his one cup of coffee.

"It's good," Annabelle said as she clamped on her ball cap and pulled her ponytail out the back. "The cause of most crashes is hitting the earth . . . so up we go."

Even though they were not flying that morning, Bobby and Esther Myrtle came into the bar while the travelers were eating. Bobby looked pale and sick to his stomach. Esther was excited and her cheeks were pink.

"I told you yesterday that she packed a hell of a lot of her stuff. But this morning I discovered that she took her passport, for God's sake. Why would she pack her passport if she was being kidnapped? My god, people, what is going on?" Venus's mom said.

Everyone sitting around that early breakfast table shook their heads, not knowing what to say. Finally, Ellie spoke up. "She was wearing my scarf when she left."

"What?" Mrs. Myrtle said, tired, scared, and confused.

"When I saw her yesterday, she was wearing the scarf that was stolen from our apartment."

The entire group seemed to let out a collective sigh, as if all of them at once were reconsidering the wisdom of the flight and the problematic rescue.

◙ ◙ ◙

THE NIGHT ON board the *Phalarope* had been eventful.
It was a fine old wooden ship. The timbers were sound
throughout. The planking had seen some years, but as long
as she stayed off the rocks, Venus felt that she would stay
together. The ship had a thick double set of cedar planking,
with oak ribs and heavy bracing. Whenever the *Phalarope* was
out of the water for painting or repairs, George liked to say
that she was a "fine old slab, whose keel was as straight as a
new pool cue."

Venus knew her way around the boat, having taken several
trips with George and her own family. She claimed the small
cabin in front of the bulkhead to the keel-deep hold where
the bodies had been slung and secured. Dot followed her
everywhere she went. The Southerners had warned Venus
that if the dog made a move they didn't like, they would
put her—Dot—over the side. But as she thought about it,
she couldn't be sure they were not talking about her. There
were several obvious places to store gear in her little cabin.
She found a tiny door at the bottom of the forward closet.
When you opened the little hatch, there was a small aperture
leading straight down to the hull where the through-hull
electronic gear for the depth-sounder was set in place. There
was a small box around the transponder. That is where she
hid the handgun George had given her.

Then she took out two of the drawers that were built into
the structure of her bunk. She took the large bag containing
her clothes and placed it next to the curved hull in back
and beside the drawers. This way someone who was looking
would only see an empty drawer.

While the boat traveled down the inlet, the waves were neither too big nor too steep. Venus went through a small door
to the hold and grabbed a sling net, which George used to
hoist gear on board. She found a large spool of green twine
on a workbench. She flipped on a light and found a knife

to cut the twine. In the throbbing light, the coffin sat in the bottom of the hold tied down to struts mounted on the ribs of the boat. George had insisted that it be secured tightly. In the weather to come, the light wooden box could bang itself to shreds if not heavily secured. Venus put another rope across the top and held it down with a knot she had learned as a child. Blood seeped from the seams in the box and dripped down into the bilge.

She came back up the steps and out on the back deck with the netting and the knife.

"What the heck are you doing with that knife, little missy?" Spangler's voice was still thin and full of fear. Yet he continued to act demanding.

"I'm going to secure some webbing on the back deck. If we have to get out on the deck to offload the launch in rough seas, we will need sure footing. Can't be slipping and sliding around out there in rough weather."

He stared at her and thought for a moment. The wind was not as harsh with the boat going downwind, but it still whistled through the rigging holding the boom and winch mast in place.

"Okay," he yelled over the wind. "But you put that knife back in the sink when you come in. I'll be watching you, young woman."

The netting was about twelve feet square, and it took Venus about half an hour to get it tightly laced on the deck. She didn't cut herself with the knife, even though the seas were beginning to build as they neared the western mouth of the inlet toward the open sea. They would likely go north and then turn back to the east once they got to the second inlet toward the inside waters. George knew all the little otter trails through the rocks and bays to shorten the passage on the outside, but Venus doubted these Southerners could read George's pencil markings on the chart or had enough courage to take the *Phalarope* that close to the crashing rocks. They would likely go offshore away from the rocks and then make a difficult turn into the trough to get back toward the inside waters. That short passage in the trough of the big seas would not look bad on the chart, but she knew it would be harrowing and uncomfortable if either of them were prone to seasickness.

She went back into the cabin. Put the knife in the sink.

"Make us some food!" Atz yelled at her. She could see that he was scared and needed to be a jerk to build himself up.

"I'm not going to make food. We need to get everything fastened down. When we get out there a little farther, things are going to start flying around. I'm going to make sure the anchor and the winch boom are secure. Stuff flying around out there can sink a boat. Then I'm going to get my own stuff safe, so it doesn't all break apart. I suggest you do the same."

She tried to make sure Dot stayed in the cabin, but the big dog would not leave her side. There were lines stowed out by the winch boom she needed. Venus and Dot scrambled out onto the heaving bow, which was beginning to dip low enough toward the oncoming waves to soak her and the dog to the bone. Dot barked hard into the storm. Venus grabbed the dog's collar, and when she stumbled, the one-hundred-pound dog put her weight into Venus's and kept her on her feet. In this way they got the anchor and chain latch secure. Venus had heard stories of anchors coming loose in storms and being thrown through the front of a boat and into the operator's lap.

Then she lashed the launch, which was sitting in its cradle behind the hatch cover in the stern. Venus used a third chain for this and used a heavy turnbuckle to tighten it, then secured the chain together with two shackles. The chain might tear up the finish on the smaller boat, but she was certain that George would much prefer some scratches to losing his prize launch.

They were heading toward the outside, and the waves were building to over ten feet cresting on top of the high rolling swells. The two Southerners looked at the charts and talked about the course. Venus grabbed a towel and dried herself off. She looked around to see that they had put the dishes away in the cabinet after they made themselves peanut butter sandwiches. The rest of the pilothouse was far from squared away for rough seas. The *Phalarope* was lunging now: riding up the oncoming swells and crashing up through the curling chop at the peak of the waves and smashing down into the troughs. The plates in the cabinets were clattering around in their holders. The trash can, which had not been stowed, had tipped over. Binoculars were on the floor and the teapot rolled across the decking and clattered into the pocket door amidships. It would be messy and loud in the storm, but as long as they kept her into the seas and off the rocks, the ship would hold together. There was nothing more she could do until the next unexpected thing happened. Which it surely would. She would know by the sound and the motion, then she would help their ignorant souls.

"I'm going below," Venus said. "You guys are going to get beaten to death up here."

She helped Dot outside and held on to her firmly as the dog peed into the scuppers along the side. After a hard roll, she knew that Dot would be sick and most likely have diarrhea, but that was a problem for another time. She got Dot down into her compartment, strung some storm webbing over the opening of her bunk, and then got in the narrow bunk with the dog, who was being held snugly in place by the webbing. Her plan was to ride out the storm there.

She had a hard stomach and had not been seasick since she had been in kindergarten. She dozed as best she could, imagining where they were headed. If the fools could get out past the rocks and offshore and not break apart, they would be fine. If they tried to go inside using radar and the LORAN navigation system, then they might be in trouble because they were likely to smash into the hard edge of the continent.

Venus lost track of time, with the lulling sound of the

engine underneath the floor and the stable singing of the wind through the rigging. She shoved Dot farther down so she could lay her shoulders flat on the bunk without getting her face too close to Dot's mouth. As the *Phalarope* lurched harder into the seas, Dot began panting with her long red tongue lolling out of her mouth. If Venus came too close, Dot would lick her in the face and on the ear.

"Silly dog." Venus laughed and pushed her farther down. Both of them were well settled in and had gotten a little sleep when Dot was the first to notice the sudden change in the atmosphere of the boat. The engine did not sputter or glug but simply stopped running. Dot barked and wanted out immediately. The *Phalarope* slid down the face of the next swell and began to turn broadside to the waves. All forward momentum was gone. The *Phalarope* was floundering.

In a moment, Venus was in the pilothouse.

"What did you do?" she asked.

"We didn't do a thing. The damn thing just stopped," Spangler screeched back at her indignantly, as if she were the cause of their problems. Venus missed the sound of the engine now. The boat was filled with the slap of waves and the roar of the wind.

The sun was still up and they were not past the mass of coastal rocks near shore. Waves crashed on rocks not a hundred yards from the direction the ship was drifting. Gravity of the big seas gripped all their bodies. Atzerodt kept grinding on the starter motor as the lights began to dim.

"Stop doing that!" Venus yelled. "It's not going to start and you are running the battery down."

"Are you going to listen to this girl?" Spangler said. "How do we know she didn't do something to the engine? Some sabotage?"

Atz turned to Venus. He had taken a good, deep breath. "Now, Venus, do you know how to get the motor running? Please tell me if you do." Atz was showing genuine fear.

"Come with me," she said. "I know one thing, but if it

doesn't work, we will have to abandon ship. You don't want to risk that on this chunk of coast." She pointed to Spangler. "Don't crank it anymore. Turn off all the power."

Then she walked out onto the dangerously rolling deck that was going from side to side, lurching wildly now rather than pitching forward into the waves. Atz was behind her.

"Big diesel engines don't stop like that unless they are not getting fuel or not getting air."

By the winch mast was a ladder and a hatch through the decking. She pulled the door and climbed down into the hold. There was the coffin and the workbench. There were buckets, tools, and, most importantly, a large silver flashlight. Toward the bow was the door to the engine room.

"If the engine is underwater, then it's not getting air. If that's what's happening, nothing we can do before we hit the rocks."

She opened the door to the engine room. There was another hatch from above, which was the more usual way to get to the engine, but she needed the supplies.

"The more common thing to happen is for the filters to get plugged when you get into rough seas and all the algae and other gunk in these old tanks gets stirred up and plugs the filters. If the contamination is worse, then the gunk plugs the injectors, and that's really complicated to fix. Let's just hope it's the filter."

"We change the filter?"

"Yes, I've helped George do this."

The engine room was hot, but it was not full of water.

"Just hold the flashlight for now. The tanks are fairly full." The great red engine seemed forlorn, like a hot sweaty race-horse that had come to a dead stop, steam rising from its hide. There was the smell of oil in the bilge, and the motion of the boat floundering in such an unnatural way caused Atzerodt to get almost instantly sick.

Venus was able to slide a bucket under the float and crack it open at the top and the bottom.

"Wait . . ." she almost shouted. "I have to turn off the fuel supply." She lowered the valve arm, and gas stopped leaking from the top of the filter bowl. She opened a small box and replaced the filter, putting the used one in the bucket with the dirty fuel.

Mr. Atzerodt threw up into the bilge.

"Hold that light steady—oh just give it to me." She went forward toward the flywheel of the great red engine. She had a wrench and cracked a nut open.

"Now, see that little flippery thing on the side of the engine next to that other metal filter? The one without a bowl? No, that one."

Atz vomited again, this time on the engine. The bucket with the dirty engine fuel started to tip over and slide toward the stern. The oil splashed out onto Atz's pants and the smell overwhelmed him.

"You are doing good. Now hold the bucket and at the same time pump that flipper up and down. We've got to make sure there is no air in the system."

Atz valiantly pumped, held the bucket, and puked. A few bubbles came out of the line Venus had opened, and then a steady flow poured out and on top of the hot engine. Now she was starting to get sick.

"Good, now get out of here." She tightened all the fittings, remembering George's advice not to horse them down too hard or else she would break or strip something. She said his words of advice aloud. "Don't horse the hardware: lefty loosie and righty tighty, snug and firm, but never make the situation worse by stripping a fitting."

Atz made his way to the back hatch. Everything looked tight and in order. She checked the fuel level and the engine oil level. She checked the air filter, then grabbed the bucket and the tools and headed out. She threw the tools into the bucket with the oil and simply put the bucket inside another bucket that was secured to the leg of the bench. Then she made it up and out onto the deck.

The fresh stormy air was wonderful, and even though the boat was tossing hard, she felt instantly better.

"Okay," she yelled toward the pilothouse, "start the goddamn engine!" They were some eight to ten feet from the whitewater on the rocks.

The motor made a grinding sound for perhaps three seconds and then it caught and roared to life.

"Yes!" she said. "Now back carefully away from the rocks. Put the ass of the boat into the seas first. If you go forward at all you will crush the prop."

Mr. Spangler, though he hated listening to her and hated following her directions even more, backed up the *Phalarope* carefully, and slowly made a long arcing turn back into the storm.

Atz was about to sit down on the captain's chair. "Stop!" Venus yelled at him. "Change your clothes. You get that diesel on things in here, you will feel like puking the entire trip. Take your clothes off and tie them outside. Or put them in a bucket."

"Yes, sir," Atz said without sarcasm, then went out on the back deck to stand firmly and without slipping on the webbing she had laid out. He stripped off his clothes down to his underwear, all the while still retching, trying to empty his stomach.

When she got back down to her compartment, Dot was waiting for her. She let Dot into the hold where she did indeed have diarrhea. Venus made sure there was a lid on the pail of dirty oil, took the tools out, wiped them down, and put them away. She took off her own clothes and opened a through-hull valve, then washed herself off as best she could in icy-cold seawater. She cleaned up Dot's mess by rinsing everything down into the interior scuppers.

Then she sat naked on the dark hold just a doorway from her bunk and gear, and cuddled the big dog in her arms. "Oh, Dot," she said in between dog kisses, "you poor baby."

◉ ◉ ◉

THE BIG PLANE was full: two up front—Ellie and Anna-belle were the pilots—George and Glen behind them, then the brother and Slip with survival gear and the brother's bags in the very back. The brother had decided to pay for the flight, so Annabelle could see some profit from this adven-ture, and so she would take him to whatever port he could make it out of.

The sun was coming down into the bottom of the inlet now, yet the day seemed to be swaddled in shadows made by clouds and rain, and made more violent by the tearing fingernails of the wind across the water. Everyone fastened their shoulder belts into the clips. Brother Louis snugged the strap almost uncomfortably tight. The de Havilland Beaver had a wing-over configuration and in the snout was a powerful radial engine; the bulk of it almost sat right in the pilot's lap. The pontoons were a stout structure holding up the plane with thick aluminum struts. The interior was pebbled gray aluminum. The Beaver was a flying military-style truck, seemingly too heavy, incredibly loud.

Ellie pushed the throttle levers open and began nosing out of the harbor into the waves. She forced the round mouth of the power plant into the wind. Annabelle gripped her yoke, put her own feet on the yaw controls.

"We can do this together, right?" She spoke to Ellie through the radio headset. "Don't fight each other, trust each other's instinct. We can do this, right?"

"Yes. I won't jerk it out of your hands. Don't worry, doll," Ellie said with a thin smile.

The waves began to porpoise the plane across the surface. Annabelle put her hand over Ellie's on the throttle.

"If we aren't fully in the air by the time we clear the point, power down," Annabelle said.

Ellie nodded. "Roger that."

"Here we go then," said Annabelle, and they put both hands down on the throttle.

George pulled his belt tight. Glen took a breath but was not tense; he simply felt happy because no one would be shooting jacketed bullets through the thin aluminum sheeting of the fuselage.

The heavy plane was sluggish in the water. Then it bounced on top of the waves. Hard hits. Shaking the passengers' guts. The plane felt lighter and the rattling of the washboard ride became easier and more shallow. The pontoons were planing on top of the sea, but the Beaver stayed stuck to the surface. The brother could feel the aft portion of the floats staying stuck in the water. The point of land by the island at the mouth of the harbor was coming closer. Beyond that point, the tops of waves were blown into smoke. The last section of the pontoon lifted off as they passed the point. They were in the air by inches. Then a magnificent gust grabbed the wings and stood the airplane on its tiptoes. The windscreen was full of sky. The plane had gone off the ramp of a big wave and tried to crawl into the air, but because it was facing straight up, the propeller was too weak to pull it up, and the wind was pushing it over backward as the engine screamed.

Both women pushed the throttle forward. The weight of the Beaver was sinking the pontoons, and as they were about to be blown over, Annabelle gave the throttle just enough punch at the last second to right the plane, allowing it to fall forward as the back of the pontoons were going under the waves. It fell and dipped its right wing straight into an oncoming wave, which spun the plane around with the tail into the wind.

The torque of the motion had jerked the steering yokes out of Annabelle's and Ellie's hands, but the Beaver was upright, no alarms were blaring, and it bobbed on the surface of the sea comically like a rubber duck.

No one said a word as Annabelle steered the Beaver back into the harbor and slowly, gently back to the seaplane ramp. When she was standing on the dock in her silky pilot's jacket,

Annabelle's hands were shaking. Ellie clambered out of the plane and hugged her niece.

"You are the best goddamn pilot I've ever seen," Ellie whispered in her ear.

"For crashing my plane in the first ten seconds of flight?" Annabelle asked.

"For getting us back to shore in one piece."

"We will wait for the weather to improve. I don't know what I was thinking."

"*Lord Jesus Christ, Son of God, have mercy on me, a sinner.*"

The brother stood, pale and mumbling, on the floatplane dock. "Is the bar open?" he asked.

# 13
# LYNN CANAL

The Southerners decided to get to the inside waters and head north. That way they could get onto the road system and into Canada quickly. Once in Skagway, they could find a truck and be in Whitehorse, Canada, in just a few hours. There was a mine just across the border, and they knew men working there who were sympathetic to their cause. They also had a man in the border and customs offices of both countries.

The *Phalarope* was, in fact, a good old slab with a fine stern and a straight keel, which took well to following seas. Storm winds eased up during the night, particularly offshore, where they stayed most of the night. The Southerners had gotten Slippery to show them how to use the LORAN plotter, which would give them coordinates they could plot on a chart, so they could stay away from rocks they could not see at night.

By morning they were able to calculate a course into Icy Strait and avoided any hazards. The ocean swells rolled long and slow, but the wind chop had died down, so the old slab would ride down the swell without wanting to turn sideways to the sea. But, still, the boat shifted and moved erratically when they were inattentive to the helm.

After her shower and a good nap, Venus and Dot came up into the pilothouse and offered to do a three-hour shift at the helm. If all three of them did three hours, they could each get six hours of sleep, something the Southerners desperately needed.

Atz settled on the bunk in the pilothouse, and Spangler started to go below. Then he turned back and put both hands around Venus's waist.

"You obviously are good with this boat. Just don't try anything funny, or you won't make it home alive."

"Nothing funny. I understand," she said.

Spangler pulled her in close from behind. She was already standing at the helm, scanning the gauges and the horizon ahead.

She could feel the hardness in his crotch and stepped away. "Come on now, darlin'. Don't be like that," he whispered. "I know you don't want to be with the fat man, but we could be good together," he said straight into her right ear, his hands wriggling up under her shirt.

"Dot, OW!" she said loudly and pulled away.

Dot's ears perked up, and the big dog looked at the two of them standing together. "OW!" Venus said again. "Dot, OW!"

The big dog bolted up off the deck and flung herself at Mr. Spangler's upper thigh. Dot was able to get the man's entire right buttock between her jaws, and bore down. She made a throaty groan but did not break the skin with her canine teeth. She did not pull him to the deck as she easily could have. She did not thrash her head and neck side to side in order to rip off a hunk of meat as she could have. She just clamped down on Spangler's largest muscle and held on to it, waiting for Venus's next words.

"Now back up slowly," Venus said, "and we will let you keep that ass cheek."

Dot and Mr. Spangler backed up slowly.

Once he was out of reach, Venus said, "I'm okay, Dottie. Thank you." The dog let him go, walked around the man, then sat down at the girl's feet and stared at the defeated conspirator. Dot's expression was somewhat sad, as if she was disappointed in how things had turned out.

"Ooooh, thank you, sweetie," Venus said as she scratched Dot's ears. "Good dog. Good, good dog."

Atzerodt was chuckling from the captain's daybed when Mr. Spangler went below to find a bunk.

DURING THE HEIGHT of the storm the phone lines were down. One time the power went out in Cold Storage, but the citizens got it up and running again quickly in the morning. The telephones were line-of-sight relays and people in town did not have a clue where the break in the link was. After their harrowing attempted takeoff, the brother and Glen ate at the café one more time. They discussed the future and their happiness that they were still alive.

"I got a letter from the army a couple of weeks ago. They want to interview me again," Glen said as he ate his BLT.

"What are you going to do?" the brother asked.

"What do you think I should do? I mean, what is the good thing to do? I'm not going to change anything by talking to anyone, am I?"

"I don't mean to cop out on you, Glen, but I think you should do what your conscience dictates. If it were me, I would pray. But if that doesn't work for you, just think about what the long-term effect on your soul will be if you don't talk."

"Long term . . ." Glen said aloud but as if to himself. "To tell you the truth, Brother, I don't know if I have any long term . . . I don't mean I'm going to kill myself. I don't know, I just don't feel . . . invested in the future at all. It's like I have a loud horn blaring in my skull whenever I think about the war and what I saw there. I just want to turn it off."

"What do you want, Glen? What do you want to happen?"

Just then, Deedee brought the brother's fish and chips and a soda, putting a small pause on the conversation, one Glen needed in order to think of an answer.

"I want it to stop."

"The horn, the war, your memories?" Thomas Merton, the enemy of the United States, put ketchup on his food.

"All of it," Glen said. "I know it sounds crazy, but some-times I think of going back to Vietnam. I'm there in my mind all the time anyway."

"I know a writer. A very good journalist. He writes for important publications. He is also a very good investigator. Talk with him if you want. Ask him what he thinks. I'm not saying it will help you necessarily, but this writer would make sure that your story was not simply covered up." The brother slid a page from his notebook with a name, address, and tele-phone number over the table and under Glen's fingertips.

"And what does this do?" Glen asked with genuine sadness in his voice.

"The truth comes out. Perhaps the army changes what they ask of their men."

"Brother, I doubt that."

"Or at least it would disturb the people who think that they have the power to keep such things secret."

"Now you are talking," and for the first time in days, Glen Andre smiled.

THE NEXT MORNING the storm had abated. George Hanson had gotten a radio call on the flight service channel that the *Phalarope* had been seen headed up Lynn Canal toward either Haines or Skagway. They were about twenty miles south of Haines.

Annabelle had winched her plane up onto the dock and had gone over the rigging of the pontoons. She tightened struts and made sure there was no water leaking into the floats. She wiped down the engine with cleaner and oil, making sure the salt water, which had blown in through the cowling, was not crusting up. She changed all the filters that she could, then turned over the engine and let it idle. She wanted to listen to it to make sure it ran smoothly. She had a fuel caddy and let that run for hours. The Beaver had no irreparable damage and sounded strong as all the pistons fired.

Ellie came down to help them load. "You don't need an

old woman on this flight," she told Annabelle and George at the dock. Ellie looked at the brother and George for several seconds, then after she had made her decision to tell them, she said, "Three people came in last night and said there was stuff missing from their house—cash, some jewelry. One person reported that a box and a half of his nine-millimeter pistol ammunition had been taken. They figure it was taken the day before yesterday, just before the *Phalarope* left town in the storm."

"All right," George said.

"Why would that girl need ammunition, George?" Ellie asked.

"Why don't we try and bring her back and ask her," George said.

Bobby Myrtle came into the office. "I really want to go with you on this trip," he said as he took off his rain jacket and patted down his waterproof waxed canvas pants to knock the water off. "I can pay Venus's and my way back."

Annabelle shook her head in agreement. "Okay," was all she said.

"I've heard the rumors about things being taken. I just want to go get her and bring her back."

"Sounds right," George said.

THE TAKEOFF WAS uneventful this time, and the ride, while not perfectly smooth, did not bring on that gut-grinding grip of fear that the brother was expecting. Islands lay equitably in the sea, and the waves broke like the manes of wild horses against the rocks. A few boats began to poke out of little inlets in their hunt for salmon, and clouds rode the sky like battle wagons. The brother said a prayer for Ellie and Slip just after he hugged them goodbye.

"Do you want your mummy back?" George had asked Ellie before he climbed the pontoons.

"Just bring the girl back. That's all I care about," she had said.

◎ ◎ ◎

LYNN CANAL WAS calming down. The Chilkat mountains were white with new snow on top. The wind was backing now, not making any surface chop. Soon the weather would be coming from the north; a stiff wind would lift snow on the cornices up high like silk scarfs fluttering off the mountains. They saw only two fishing boats and a tug heading north toward the terminus of the Inside Passage.

Soon enough the *Phalarope* came into view. The big boat sat in a small indentation in the fjord, some four miles from Skagway. The boat was hidden from the view of town and was riding at anchor. The first thing George noticed was that the launch was not in its cradle and the winch boom was deployed over the port side of the boat. The second thing he noticed was that Dot was tied up with a line to her collar on the back deck.

"I don't think anyone is on the boat," George said, "besides Dot."

They scanned up the Lynn Canal toward Skagway and could not see the launch.

"Can you buzz the boat and see if we get some reaction out of them? I mean, if they are serious about killing the girl, at this point they would wave us off."

Annabelle swung down and flew about fifty feet above the deck and tipped her wings as she passed the *Phalarope*. There was no one running out on the back deck, no one waving a pistol around or holding it to the head of a teenage girl. George could see that Dot was barking at the plane as its engine blared past.

"Put it down and let's take a look," George told Annabelle through his headset.

THEY SET THE plane down and pulled up to the stern. George went on board first with his rifle cradled in his arms. He moved slowly as he checked out the boat, then came back and signaled the others to join him.

Bobby Myrtle came off first, and George said, "She's not here. Look through the boat and see if you can find any message . . . anything from your daughter."

Bobby Myrtle took off and went inside. The brother was next to clatter aboard. Annabelle decided to stay on the Beaver, not wanting to trust the knot-tying of the others to keep her plane safe.

"What did you find?" the brother asked George.

"I don't know," George said. "Keep this to yourself, okay, Brother? Don't tell Venus's father until I figure something out."

"Sure . . . but . . ."

"Come look." George touched the brother's elbow and pointed as they walked to the side. "Blood in the scuppers. Someone tried to clean it up but missed down low on the hull. See that red stain? That's a lot of blood. Then here, where there was some netting on the deck." The brother could see a dirty blood-colored checkerboard pattern where George was pointing.

"They tried to clean this up too, but . . . you never really get it all." George walked over to the wriggling dog and undid the line attached to her collar. Dot went wild, pushing into George and giving him licks on his face.

"Oh, yes, yes," George said as he sat down on the hatch cover, holding the dog's face in his hands. "Yes, I'm glad to see you too."

He looked up at the brother and said, "Go ahead and look around. Try not to touch anything with your hands, but just tell me where you see blood or if you notice anything odd. Okay? I'm going to calm this dog down." Like many adult men who live alone with their dogs, George was not going to acknowledge just how grateful and happy he was to find Dot alive on his boat.

Down in the engine room, just below where the netting had lain on the deck, blood had seeped through the floor-boards. It had even dripped down onto the top of the alternator and spattered back onto the ceiling. There were blood droplets in the hold that no one had tried to clean up. There were smears of blood on the winch handles, which had been wiped with something. But whoever had tried to hide the evidence had left blood to pool near the hinge of the lever, where it was harder to get to; or perhaps the blood had seeped out after the attempted cleanup. The entire process of wiping up blood had been rushed.

The obvious things were missing: the makeshift coffin was gone, and there appeared to be no personal belongings, backpacks or luggage, left on the boat. Then, as the brother sat down by George and Dot, he noticed that someone had left a big bag of dog food open on the deck with a bucket of fresh water brimming full within the dog's reach. But what really caught the brother's attention was that someone had rigged a tarp above the deck with a hose to collect the rain to drain straight into the big dog's water bucket.

"So, what do you think?" the brother asked the old cop.

"I don't think those Southern boys would go to the trouble to make sure this old hound would have enough food and water until we got here."

The brother let George's words sink in.

"We should go to town and find the launch and look around for the girl. But I don't think we're going to find her."

"What about the two men?" the brother asked.

"We're definitely not going to find them," was all George said.

# 14

# DHARMSHALA

*The milk of the lioness is so precious and so powerful that if you
put it in an ordinary cup, the cup breaks.*
—Tibetan saying, noted in Thomas Merton's
journal on November 1, 1968

The feeling of being in Dharmshala was that of being on a progression of mountains. It was early October and Thomas Merton stood on a hill looking up toward a high mountain ridge, beyond which lay mountain peaks. But beyond those peaks lay the tallest, most beautiful mountain range he had ever seen. The Himalayas seemed to levitate in the distance, or perhaps they were suspended from Heaven itself.

The temperature on October 1 was in the low sixties. His hotel room was cold and rain had just cleared the sky of the coal dust that had painted the air the weeks before. He stayed in his room wearing his warm coat for hours trying to catch up in his journal. His schedule was tight with meetings. He and his escort rode the train from Delhi to Pathankot, then traveled the rest of the way by jeep. The road was long and constantly wound uphill. Dharmshala itself was in a narrowing valley of northern India leading up toward the highlands of Tibet. It was a world of up valley and down, filled with construction and the atmosphere of constant gathering and departing. For the Tibetans who still gathered by the thousands every year to be near the Dalai Lama, this was a holy encampment where they came to wait for His Holiness to get their country back from the Communist Chinese.

On his first day there, Father Merton, as he was known formally to others, happened to be walking one of the miles of sidehill paths on the edge of the pine forests where he met by chance a man who introduced himself as Sonam Kazi. Thomas Merton recognized the name as belonging to a famous interpreter and translator of sacred Tibetan texts. Kazi had been walking with a lama, and was happy to let the lama go on his way so that Kazi could join Father Merton for tea in a café a few hundred meters down the path.

They walked slowly and in silence for a time, enjoying the moments of their walk. Kazi wore a dark Western suit and tie. The father had been advised to wear his snow-white Cistercian robe and black bib-like scapular, "so as not to be confused with the ordinary European tourist," his friend had told him. It was much better to be seen as an "American lama" than a common trekker, or a soldier on vacation.

Lyndon Johnson, who was not standing for election that coming November, had stopped all bombing of Vietnam in order to demonstrate America's willingness to come to peace talks, and this suspension had been the subject of much speculation in Dharmshala. Some of the Tibetans who followed the precepts of compassion had nonetheless pinned their hopes on the United States' deadly military power in that region as a way to force the Chinese back to the topic of a free Tibet. Father Merton and the translator eventually discussed politics briefly on the way to the coffee shop. Merton couldn't help being optimistic about the halt in the bombing, but like the chill in the shadows, he was worried what would happen in the war if Richard Nixon was elected.

The valley was full of sounds: the high call of birds in the thicket, insects drumming their wings, the wind sighing through the pine and cedar forest. Car horns blew and bicycle bells on motorbikes blended with the birdsong. Dharmshala had the sounds of a forest city constantly being built. Yet, still, gunfire down in the valley where Indian troops practiced war games and the small boys danced on the streets setting off the *pop, pop, pop* of cheap fireworks could be heard amid all the other noises.

They sat at a flimsy table after ordering their tea. A small black bird pecked around their feet.

"Father?" Sonam Kazi said as he lifted his cup to his lips. "I have a young student who came to me very recently. She is very keen to meet you, and I promised her that I would ask."

"I am very heavily scheduled while I am here." Merton was apologetic. "I am pursuing my own studies, as you know. I'm very interested in your work and am delighted to make more room in the day's events to speak with you at length . . ." Father Merton bowed to a Tibetan who bowed to him along the path, holding his hands' palms together as he leaned forward. "But I get so many requests to meet with these poets who press their childish poems upon me. It breaks my heart to put them off. See, it has gotten really difficult when I have so much I want to do here."

"She said that you may be hard to find, but she insisted that I give you this." He slid a folded piece of paper across the table.

When Merton opened it, he read: *You didn't happen to bring Dot with you? I am so hoping to see you.* And at the bottom of the paper was a single *V*, written with an extravagant flourish.

"What did you say her name was?" Thomas Merton asked.

"Oh, her name is Cynthia. She likes to say it's just like John Lennon's wife."

"Yes," Thomas Merton said, his voice weakened a bit by the strong tea, "I will make time to see her." He put the note in his pocket and stared down into the blackness of his cup.

FATHER MERTON SAW her coming down a path toward him. There were colorful Tibetan-style houses on her left side and a gully full of cedar trees on her left. Birdsong seemed to accompany her. She was wearing a dark winter coat one might see on a ski hill and a colorful knit hat with a large tassel on top. Venus was smoking a cigarette, holding it in her small ungloved hands. When she saw she was approaching the same little café where the father had met with the translator who arranged the meeting, she stopped, spit in her hand, put her cigarette out in her palm, put the butt in her pocket, then wiped her hand off with a colorful bandana.

She walked up to him quickly and kissed him twice, once on each cheek, as he stood up. She smelled of tobacco and of a popular peppermint soap favored by young travelers.

"It is wonderful to see you. You are the reason I am here," she said, then stopped speaking and just looked at him standing there, possibly to assess his attitude upon seeing her. He was skeptical but smiling.

"I'm the reason?" the father said. "I would think being wanted by police back in Alaska would have been a good enough reason to run so far from there."

A skinny dog trotted down the path and stopped to sniff Venus's hand, and she petted its ears. "May I sit?" she asked, but immediately did so without waiting for his reply.

The dog trotted on after sensing there was no food coming. "Have you news of my parents?"

"I have heard that they are both worried sick," the father said. "I must say I'm impressed that you have made it so far so quickly."

"I had money. They had fifty thousand dollars in that case." She ordered tea and warm bread with butter and jelly. The father ordered the same.

"I have been praying for you," he said. "If you didn't simply murder those men, I don't see any reason for you to not stay on the boat and explain what happened. Why did you run?"

The song of the mountain birds clattered like the old carousel music along the boardwalk of Cold Storage. Two young men in well-worn trekking clothes bowed to Venus in recognition. She simply waved with three fingers of her left hand.

The two other American-looking men who appeared to know Venus wore khaki pants and short-sleeve shirts. About twenty yards behind the travelers were two other men with flat-top haircuts and black-rimmed glasses who were taking pictures of Father Merton and Venus. Thomas Merton had seen men dressed much like this photographing him all during his trip through Asia.

"All I have wanted for the last few years was to leave that place—and that horrible little town," she said. "The police would have taken their money away from me. My parents would have made me come home."

"You seemed happy there."

"Oh my God . . ." She put sugar in her tea. "My parents were controlling freaks and there was no real life to look forward to there—eating fish and chips and drunks playing funny music. There was nothing for me there."

"Did you murder those two men?"

"So now you have love and compassion for those two? They were horrible. Yes, I killed them, but it was not murder."

"How did you decide that they didn't deserve to live? This is what troubles my prayers."

She set her teacup down hard enough to rattle her saucer. "My mom made me take birth control pills, and these breasts got so big. I know what men think about when they look at me." Anger was rising in her voice.

"Why did she make you take the pills?"

"Truthfully, I think she was worried that my father would get me pregnant."

"Was that possible?"

"We never had sex, but I'm telling you he was obsessed with me. He documented every second of my life. He drew pictures of me naked, even as I started going through puberty. He kept saying that it was beautiful and 'natural.' There was nothing dirty about the body if you didn't have dirty thoughts in your mind."

"Did he have these dirty thoughts about you?" Father Merton asked.

"I don't know. I wanted him to stop drawing me. I wanted to love my own body. I didn't want *him* loving it. It was creepy."

"What did your mother say?"

"Please . . . She had no options. She talked about moving and finding her own life, but as time went on, I swear they both became afraid of the world outside. She was convinced that he would stop, but if anyone in the real world found out what was really going on in our family, we would all be separated. She said we lived outside of society life, and that was it. So let me ask you, would Cold Storage, Alaska, be enough for you FOREVER?"

"So you started stealing?"

"Just small things, small amounts. I'm sure that everybody knew. All the people like the women at the restaurant, all the people who didn't hate all the outside cannery workers." She spread butter on her bread. She drank a sip of tea and stared down at her feet.

"Thomas . . . Father Merton, let me tell you that the saddest day of my year was when those cannery workers left to go home. Left me there in Cold Storage while they all went back to the world with movies and music and real friends, to learn and read all kinds of other stuff that wasn't all about preserving food or tearing down an engine."

"Why didn't you tell anyone else about your frustration, Venus?"

"Everyone said just to wait. Wait. Look at Glen. He waited and got drafted and now all he wants to do is sit in that bar and drink."

"Glen was taken away, you know?"

"No. Did he get in trouble about that boat stuff?"

"Not exactly. I got a letter from Ellie saying the army came to Juneau and then out to Cold Storage and asked him to go back to DC. The army wanted to know who else knew about what happened in those villages. Someone started talking to the press. The army investigators wanted to know everything he knew."

"Is he in jail?" She looked genuinely concerned.

"No, he is staying at a nice hotel with a good expense allowance. It covers everything but alcohol. Ellie said Glen was trying to quit drinking."

"Poor Glennie," was all she said to that.

"Tell me what happened on the boat, Venus." The father spoke softly and leaned toward her. "I could even hear your confession, and that way I could not testify against you."

"Confession?" She looked at him sadly.

"No matter what happened, I think . . . I believe you need to tell someone the truth."

"But really, you couldn't testify against me?"

"Just tell me you are a Catholic now. Just tell me to forgive you and that you haven't been to confession since the end of August."

And she did.

APPARENTLY AS THE *Phalarope* approached Haines, the Southerners became more and more agitated. There were some whispered discussions about what they could do. Venus tried to feign sleep, but they discussed taking her with them all the way back to Alabama, and they discussed a "fish-food solution." This went on for hours. They were going to rent a truck in Skagway and drive to Whitehorse, then fly to Vancouver and on to Seattle. Then consider taking a train. They would leave the rental truck in Whitehorse if possible, without raising suspicion, or return the truck to Skagway and one of them would find their way back to Whitehorse on their own. They also considered just giving Venus the truck in Canada and letting her deal with the problems. She didn't know their real names, only their Lincoln Conspirator names. They were going to find a place to stop just short of Skagway and get rid of Boston Corbett's body via the "fish-food solution." The final decision about what to do with Venus was left up in the air, when Venus helped them find a place on the chart to base their disposal activities.

Spangler very much wanted to have sex with her. He couldn't keep his hands or his eyes off of her. He even spoke of her as breeding stock back in Alabama. They got to the cove where George and the brother found the *Phalarope*, the day before the storm started to break up. Venus let the chain on the anchor run but didn't show them how to set the anchor deep into the mud. Setting the hook would make it hard for her to get the anchor back on board if she had to do it by herself.

Dot had been protective of Venus. When Spangler tried to grab her, the dog would lunge. Once, when standing on the webbing she had placed on the deck, Spangler came close and said, "We'll be leaving soon, darlin'. Come on, just give me a goodbye kiss." He crowded close to her. Then Dot growled and lunged. The dog bit him on the biceps, and she bit down hard.

"You fucking bitch," Spangler yelled, and took his revolver out of his belt, pointed it into the dog's ear, and pulled the hammer back.

Venus shot Spangler in the head with the nine-millimeter automatic that George had given her. She had kept it in her jacket pocket that day.

The pilothouse door flew open, and George Atzerodt came lunging toward her like a bear. He had something in his hands, which she thought was a gun but turned out to be a pair of binoculars. She shot him through his heart.

Both men lay on the webbing, bleeding out. Each of them had spasmodic jerking in their limbs as they died. Dot barked loudly each time one of them twitched.

After that it was a matter of initiating the "fish-food solution." She started the *Phalarope*'s engine so the hydraulic winch would work. She lowered the launch into the water to give her room to swing the winch around. She made two bundles. One for the two bodies of the recently dead. She

used line along with some old zincs she found in the hold
to weigh the bundles down. She loaded all their clothes with
them but kept aside the recruitment box. The mummy in
the coffin and the former FBI agent went into a separate
bundle along with an old starter motor, which was also in
the hold. The hardest part for her was offloading the bodies.
Atz was too heavy to move an inch by herself. She rigged
some pulleys and ropes to move him into a canvas sheet she
could tie just like she tied up the fish coolers. First she considered using the winch to lower the big bundles into the
launch, but she didn't have enough strength to roll either
bundle out of the launch. Instead, she raised the anchor on
the *Phalarope* and took all the bundles and the coffin out
into deep water. It was still windy from the storm, and the
deck rolled as the boat swung sideways into the wave action
that still came in with some strength from the south. She
found the release clip along with its attached line, which
would allow her to drop a load without setting it down for
slack, but she had a hard time figuring out the mechanism.
As the winch boom picked up the coffin and swung it out
over the side in water that was about a hundred fathoms
deep, the *Phalarope* swung and dipped awkwardly into the
trough of the sea. Venus couldn't get the package to drop.
She tried to cut the line holding the package, and in the panic
of the swinging and thumping against the hull, the coffin
cracked open, then the netting split, and the coffin floated
away downwind.

She recalled the winch and got the release to work,
allowing for a more successful deployment of the second
bundle. When she set the engine on autopilot into the wind,
she had a more stable platform to allow for the sinking of
the two Southerners' bodies in the deep water. She got back
to the anchorage, and after some panicky maneuvering she
got the anchor chain down and set the anchor deeply in
the bottom by backing the boat against the hook. Then she
bailed the launch and put a tarp over it so she would not

fill with rain. She let the rain do its work, sluicing the blood down the scuppers all night.

At sunrise she was up and doing as much cleaning as she could before she had to take the launch into town in order to catch the narrow-gauge railway up to Whitehorse. She then made a quick stop at the bank and deposited twenty-five thousand dollars in cash and hid the rest of the money inside her coat and backpack. Customs at Carcross was not very secure because of all the tourists riding the train back and forth from Skagway. She also went down by the river in Skagway about a block from the bank and scrubbed the last tiny bits of blood from her hands and clothes.

"Yes, Father, I killed those men. But I believe I had to. Not just to save Dot, but I knew that one of them was going to hurt me after he killed her. I had to do it, and I feel changed by it, but I would do it again."

As penance, the father suggested that she continue working with Sonam Kazi and begin a deep spiritual practice so that she could lose the self and overcome the suffering that he knew she still felt.

She shook her head up and down slowly. "Yes, I will. I will make you proud, Brother."

"Bring yourself peace," was all he said.

Her final act was to give him the scarf she had taken from Ellie's house and ask him to give it to the Dalai Lama. "I may never get to be in his presence," she said.

DURING HIS SECOND audience with the Dalai Lama, Father Merton discussed the girl with him and asked His Holiness about the nature of sin. They had a long talk about Karma and suffering. Thomas Merton gave the fourteenth reincarnation of the bodhisattva of compassion the girl's scarf, which she had stolen from the anarchist woman she had loved.

He tried to explain the provenance of the scarf, but the thirty-three-year-old monk only frowned slightly, as if nothing could shake him from his belief that all the drama the father related was only a slight quivering in the emptiness.

ABOUT A MONTH later, in November, Richard Nixon was elected president of the United States. On October 8, Cynthia Lennon had finally divorced John Lennon after he had left her to be with Yoko Ono, and soon enough Richard Nixon and his secretary of state continued the bombing of Cambodia and North Vietnam, all with the knowledge that the US would not, and could not, win the war there, but to appear tough to the North Vietnamese and win some concessions at the peace table to allow the plausible fiction of an American victory. No substantial concessions ever came, not even about the shape of the table at the peace talks. The North Vietnamese had become inured to death and were satisfied to wait. The war, with its growing body count for both sides, went on for six more pointless years.

Eventually the news came out about what had happened in the villages of Pinkville in the middle of March 1968. The US government tried Lieutenant Calley for the crimes, but Richard Nixon had him released on house arrest. He served three years on house arrest and then was released to go back to his home in Alabama, where the governor honored him.

Glen Andre reenlisted in the army and volunteered for helicopter duty in Vietnam. He was killed there three weeks after his deployment. In his personal belongings, his sergeant found a train ticket from Delhi to Pathankot that someone else had purchased for him.

On October 15, two bodies washed up on a beach near Skagway. One was bloated and the flesh had been partially consumed or sloughed off in the sea. The other body was strangely swathed in "ancient, leather-like skin," as if it had been preserved before going in the water. So, the murderer of the Great Emancipator continued his humiliating journey on this earth, whether his identity was actually bound to the dried-up old corpse . . . or not.

Bobby and Esther Myrtle waited for nine months to hear from their daughter, then they moved to Bellingham, where they had better communications with the outside world. Eventually Esther became a private investigator who specialized in finding runaways.

Venus Myrtle traveled throughout Asia and South America for eighteen months. In 1971 she was working as a yoga teacher in Brooklyn, New York. She had taken the name Venus Norbu and had a two-year-old son. That August she took her boy to Alaska and rode the ferry to Cold Storage. Since he was born on a Friday, the boy's name was Pemba Norbu. His father was a Sherpa from Nepal who had stayed in the high country of Nepal and never knew of his son. Pemba had frizzy black hair that stuck straight up. Venus Norbu took him into the café for ice cream and pie. Both Karen and Deedee rocked her in their arms and covered the little brown chick of a boy with kisses and tears. After an hour and a half Pemba and Venus walked back to the same ferry they had arrived in with a large box of Karen's cookies. The two of them sailed to Juneau that night, and upon Karen's suggestion, Venus bought two tickets for the next ferry to Bellingham to see her parents.

On December 10, 1968, Thomas Merton gave a lecture entitled "Marxism and Monastic Perspectives" to a group of nuns, priests, and a few lay Catholics from all over the region, at a conference center outside of Bangkok. He got through the main body of his talk and then said, "Now I'm going to disappear. I expect there will be many questions for this evening. I think we should have a Coke now."

He went back to his room, where he was found several hours later with an electric fan lying over the top of him. He was dead, apparently electrocuted. The Thai police came and took the body. The conference organizers asked about an autopsy but were told by the Thai police that if he were to be autopsied in Thailand he would have to be buried in Thailand. So no autopsy was done, and Thomas Merton's body was flown back to the Abbey of Gethsemane so he could be laid to rest by his brothers in faith. His body was flown home on a US aircraft that was bringing the bodies of American soldiers killed in Vietnam home to be buried in their own country. To this day some people believe that Thomas Merton died of a simple heart attack, others believe he was murdered by operatives of the American government.

The news of his death stunned folks in Cold Storage. Ellie Hobbes cried, but not nearly as hard as she did when she got his letter posted from India with the two pictures—one of the Dalai Lama holding her old scarf, and the other of Venus with the brother that Ellie had taken surreptitiously. In the photo Venus was smiling like a sparkling goddess out in front of the restaurant with the three-year-old Clive in her arms. There was only a short note saying, *Notice the scarf. I will tell you how I got it back when I return to CSA, which will be soon after my return to the US. Yours in solidarity, Brother Louis.*

# 15
# THE PROOF

It was black dark on the top of the ridge behind Slip and Ellie's homestead. The ponies had grazed downhill from the little pothole lake; the mare's bell had sent a deep clonking sound rising up in the darkness. The group sat close together on top—the brother, Glen, Venus, Bobby, and Esther—keeping their backs to the wind as best they could as they looked to the west. To the east the peaks of the coastal range started to appear as dark silhouettes. To the north the Fairweather Range appeared as a darkness beyond the curve of the earth. The bright pricks of light they believed in but rarely saw were the stars and planets of this particular part of the universe.

"Remember now, imagine the darkness as the primordial God. The darkness is the presence of empty being, before the creation of things," the brother said to the group. "In the darkness there was nothing, no . . . thing, no being, no light, no energy, no particle, and no wave. It was just God, the potentiality of creation. Okay?" he said.

Light seemed to be rising up from the west, below the mountains. The silhouettes began to become more defined. The stars started blinking out toward the light. Venus nodded and her eyes sparkled. The brother loved her then, in the way he loved God . . . the potentiality of creation and grace. He knew that Bobby and Esther had been smoking pot along the trail; their glittering eyes laughed at this experience.

They lived in a circus full of wonder, and the circus had just decamped on top of the ridge. Glen nodded and looked up at the stars blinking out, still lost in his despair, hoping, hoping to ease his pain.

"Watch what happens as God retreats. Watch what happens when God is driven back by the light, by the sun. Try not to think. Forget your opinions, and silence that voice inside your head that tries to narrate the story of your life. Empty your mind of any thoughts you may attempt to grab on to."

"Notice," was the last word he said as the light began to lift.

Above the western ridges, a bit of red fused with the silver in the grayness of sky. Particles from the sun arched up the dome of the world and swooped down as if they were water sluicing into the valley, purple and silver, rolling into the sky. Then slowly, shafts of silver began to break over the curve of the earth and the western peaks. These shafts of energy were like flights of silver-tipped arrows with diamond heads. Everything they struck became illuminated into detail out of the nothingness. The valley to the west blared into the focus of trees along their slopes, pointy spruce and hemlock glowing and full of green. The forest was the rich robe of a sitting monk. The rocky peaks with patches of snow suddenly appeared as the sun's light sprayed the darkness with detail. From darkness: differentia.

The group still sat in shadow as the existence swept out to the west and glittered the ocean, which was clearly a multiplicity of waves crashing against rocks and now gulls calling far off in the distance. Grass in the alpine of the peaks seemed so clear that they believed they could make out individual stems of the grasses, sedges, flowers, willows, tangled berry bushes along the slope. Deer bounded down the hill beneath them as the sun's energy seemed to be floating down out of the sky.

Then the first shaft of direct light of the sun hit them

there on their perch. Warmth and detail. Venus, smiling as if walking into the rest of her life. Bobby and Esther digging the scene. Glen, smiling now up from his grief. The brother now saw them clearly and as a collection of all their parts.

"Over there," Glen said softly and pointed to the north. There the Fairweather Range stepped forward as jagged stone peaks covered in snow. They glowed like platinum figures outlined in scarlet—the water between them glittering, the thicket below the small lake rising up in a chorus of birdsong, the warmth bringing everything into detail. A bear shambled along the tree line and ducked down toward the river valley, and the belled mare sensed the big animal, then scampered, bucking uphill for a few lazy hops, then settled down.

Soon darkness had been scoured out of the sky, but when the small group on the ridge looked straight up, the edges of what had been the bowl of night appeared to be shaded in the last eternal presence left, everything else in all its delineation lay out before them in the lap of their knowing. The rest of creation lay waiting on the other side of the globe as yet unseen. Venus began to dig through her backpack for some warm tea, which they all drank before walking off the ridge into their futures.

# AUTHOR'S NOTE

The author and Cistercian brother Thomas Merton did in fact come to Alaska in August of 1968. He did visit some small villages with thoughts of settling here. He did not come to Cold Storage, Alaska, and get involved in any such drama as I've described in the accompanying story, because I made it all up. Father Merton took the name Louis when he became a monk, and would have been known as Brother Louis in his abbey and to his friends. He was known as Thomas Merton to the lay admirers of his writing. When others who were not his brothers from Gethsemane Abbey in Kentucky referred to him formally, he was known as Father Louis; at least this is my understanding. Merton did die in Thailand in the circumstances I described.

The backstory of my character Glen Andre is based largely on the experiences of one of the witnesses to the events in Pinkville, later to be known as the My Lai massacre, which occurred in the spring of 1968. This witness was not an Alaskan and did not come home but died in combat the summer of '68. People in the United States did not hear of the My Lai massacre until 1969, thanks to the reporting of Seymour Hersh.

The rest of my characters, including the Southerners and the former FBI agent, are wholly fictitious, though there has been a long-standing conspiracy theory surrounding the events of Lincoln's assassination concerning the death of

John Wilkes Booth and the whereabouts and his corpse. Of course, there are many writings concerning the death of Martin Luther King Jr. and the role played by the FBI in his assassination, but my interpretation of those events is pure speculation.

The other characters are my own creations, and any similarity between another person living or dead is pure coincidence.

For further reading on the residents of Cold Storage, Alaska, I can recommend my earlier books, *The Big Both Ways*; *Cold Storage, Alaska*; and *What Is Time to a Pig?*, which are still in print with Soho Crime.

Information about and writings by Thomas Merton are easily found online, but his best-known book, an autobiographical memoir of his coming to faith, is *Seven Storey Mountain*. He kept detailed journals, and selections from them are still available from New Directions, including his Asian journals and his Alaskan writings. Thomas Merton clearly drew the attention of the FBI and other national security agencies during his life. While he was famous in his lifetime, his leaving Gethsemane was not prompted by the abbot as I suggested here. The thoughts and actions of the abbot were a plot device in my story. There are many opinions about the death of Father Merton in Thailand. My story does not try to confirm or deny any of these opinions. I had other goals in this tale. I can only conclude that the details of his death do seem "suspicious," at least from a straight reading of the historical record.

For information concerning what was called the Booth corpse, I recommend *The Legend of John Wilkes Booth* by C. Wyatt Evans, published by the University Press of Kansas.

As always, my thanks go out to my family—Jan, Finn, and Emily—for their support, and to Nita Couchman for her proofreading. So, too, my thanks go out to Martha Straley, Maureen Long, and Yezanira Venecia for their sensitive reading and editing of the manuscript; and all gratitude goes to my friend Yi-Fu Twan, who gave me so much to think about while writing this book.

Finally, to Dot, who lay next to the heater while I wrote this and gave me a good reason to go for frequent walks into the dense but articulated woods surrounding our house. Good dog.